Paul Mannering is an award-winning writer of speculative fiction, comedy, horror and military action novels, short stories, radio plays, and the occasional government report.

He lives in Wellington, New Zealand with his wife Damaris, and their two cats. Paul harbours a deep suspicion about asparagus and firmly believes we should all make an effort to be more courteous to cheese.

Engines of Empathy

by Paul Mannering

Engines of Empathy

All Rights Reserved

ISBN-13: 978-1-925496-88-8

Copyright ©2018 Paul Mannering

V1.0

First published in 2014.

Printed in Palatino Linotype and Voodoo Eye Title

IFWG Publishing International
Melbourne

www.ifwgpublishing.com

To Mum, thanks for everything.

PROLOGUE

As always, leaving things to the last possible minute was proving to be a bad idea. In this case, a particularly bad idea, as the last possible minute seemed certain to include the remaining moments of his life. He always expected he would die in his bed — or someone else's bed — warm, comfortable and most importantly many years hence, surrounded by descendants impatient to hear his cryptic last words. He'd given his final utterance a lot of thought and now felt a deep irritation that he would have no chance to share it with anyone.

His heavily pregnant wife had left earlier in the week to spend time with her parents before the delivery. Now he stood alone at the window of the dining room (or it may have been the parlour — his wife was the expert on such domestic details). The thunderstorm rattling the windows lit the manicured lawns with strobe-like lightning, catching the silhouette of the approaching assassin.

"So, this is how it ends," he said to the empty room. In reply, the front door of the country house exploded out of its frame. He took a moment to appreciate the prototype's remarkable strength, and to note that its fine motor skills still needed work.

He waited, a grim fascination settling on his face as he listened to the assassin searching the house. Running had its definite attractions, but as a man of science, he needed to see it, to observe the wonder of modern technology.

"Sod it," he said, and dashed on stockinged feet for his study. Easing the door shut behind him, he went to the writing desk that took pride of place in the room. It had been purchased at auction, a beautiful example of furniture made from living oak, the rare wood that had been a key to the discovery of the age. The discovery that was now going to get him killed.

The letter was complete, but there would be no time to post it now. He paused, listening between the rumbles of the storm outside for approaching death. There it was. The whirr and click of clockwork gears; the slow, deliberate sound of doom.

He folded the letter up into a narrow strip, then with shaking hands pried open the hidden slat in the roll-top desk's cover. Pressing the paper inside, he winced as the door behind him shuddered under repeated blows.

"I'll be right there!" he called. Sliding the slat back into place, he patted the desk fondly one more time and whispered, "That should cause someone no end of trouble."

Then, smiling, he went to meet his death.

CHAPTER 1

One of the many advantages of being a single, professional woman who lives alone, is there is no one around judge you on your relationships with the household appliances. So it was without feeling like a complete idiot that I stepped back from the toaster and waited until its defensive growls subsided.

It had all come down to this moment: victory for one of us and embarrassing defeat for the vanquished. I considered my next move carefully.

The appliance worked fine until you dropped slices of wholegrain bread into the slots and depressed the lever. White bread, pumpernickel, wheatmeal—none of those were ever a problem, though the toaster did burn the bottoms of crumpets (while undercooking them on the top). I had dropped English muffins and even the occasional bagel into the machine and all had emerged a few minutes later crisply toasted and otherwise unmolested.

The toaster's snarling defiance passed into silence. I gingerly reached forward and tried to pluck the cooling toast from the slots without drawing attention to myself. The growling started again, climbing the register to a higher pitch in a real tantrum of possessive fury.

"Fine!" I snapped and reached out to unplug the sunward thing. The noise ended abruptly. I snared the toast and sighed. Two thirds of the bread was gone.

My plans for a quiet morning working in the central city office, perhaps punctuated by lunch at one of the street-side cafés that served espression tea, where the flavours of empathy come with milk and sugar, were now in a state of flux. My car was in an autotherapy clinic for tests and the toaster had been getting worse. I was no longer interested in battling it each morning for breakfast.

I went to my home office, a small room under the stairs accessed through a round vault door that weighs several tonnes and requires a retina scan to unlock. The door is chrome and matt gold, with a spinning handle on it like the spokes on a ship's wheel. It was there when I moved in nine months ago. It has a state of the art eyeball-scanning security system, which for some reason refused to accept 'olive' as not a viable eye colour. Once I had managed to get the security system to accept my eyes as authorised, the room made a great place to get work done. The estate agent said the previous owner had used the space as a broom closet.

Rumbling snores choked off with a snort as I swung the vault door open. The desk coughed long and dry, setting its many drawers rattling. My desk coughs and, yes, sometimes snores gently. Not because it has a respiratory system, but because it is old, and my empathic perception of the desk gave it anthropomorphic characteristics. Could this be an explanation for my toaster's breakdown? I have never been a morning person and the first thing I did most mornings was grumpily shove bread into the appliance and slam down the lever. There are library shelves sagging under the weight of books that talk about anthropomorphic resonance, the way we relate to appliances powered with empathic energy. I resisted the sudden urge to plug my toaster back in and apologise. Personal communications always left me feeling hot faced and tongue tied.

I flicked on the light. My desk took up more space than was appropriate in the cramped room, but I had loved it since I was a little girl. My family had inherited the desk from my great-grandmother's estate. It was one of those old roll-tops lovingly crafted from rare living oak, with dozens of tiny drawers. If I put my face very close to the sun-warmed wood and inhaled gently, the smells of ancient pipe tobacco, Indian ink and patchouli oil filled my nose. The scents were a mystery to me; to the best of my knowledge my great-grandmother never smoked, wrote exclusively in pencil and never professed any interest in patchouli. The riddles of the desk were part of its appeal.

I skirted around piles of books, ducked under hanging bunches of dried computer circuitry and slid the desk open.

Each of the thirty-four drawers behind the roll-top was about the size of a playing card, and from the front of each one hung a small metal dongle like a hanging earring that served as a handle. I pulled, fossicked, and pushed closed each drawer in turn before finding the crumpled receipt for the toaster standing in for a bookmark in Benchley's *Computations in Adverse Psychology for Empathic Engineering: Pocket Edition*.

On my way out the front door I paused as briefly as possible to drop the toaster in my bag. Unplugged appliances always give me the creeps. They are so cold and still; like a small pet that has died.

The phone rang while I was locking up, so I let the machine take the call. "Hello, this is Charlotte Pudding's answering machine," the machine said, and then "No, she just left," as I stepped out into the morning sunshine and hurried to the bus stop.

My car was in one of those diagnostic clinics where you could have a doctorate in automechanical physiology but they would still leave you feeling that you didn't truly understand the seriousness of the as-yet undiagnosed problem. With the toaster banging against my thigh as I hurried down the street, I worried that my car's poor performance was my fault too. All I ever seemed to do was rush out of the house in the mornings, drive her through rush hour traffic and argue with the lyrics of the songs on the radio.

She was a red Flemetti Viscous. Dad's car originally, and one of my few possessions that gave me a sense of familial connection. It seems odd now, that I always related better to machines than to people.

I joined a dozen other morning commuters at the bus stop, catching my breath amidst the silent camaraderie of strangers forced together by the vagaries of public transport scheduling. No one felt the need to make small talk; we simply stood near each other in a calm sulk until a man strode up and fixed us with an intense glare.

"Good morning, citizens," he announced.

I glanced at him and then went back to thinking about how much the car repairs would be costing me.

"I am Vole Drakeforth, of the Williamsburg Drakeforths. Not," he assured his fellow bus-waiters, waving a long finger in the air, "of the Terracouth Drakeforths. Those other Drakeforths are syphilitic, sister-loving blaggards of the first order."

He dressed well for a lunatic, in dark pants, matching suit jacket and expensive shoes. He had shaved this morning and his eyes flashed the angry green of a police car's siren lights.

"Let me tell you about the Terracouth Drakeforths. A hideous clan of inbred custard curdlers. Born of a drunken encounter between a baboon and an Arthurian nun. The baboon was so horrified at what he had begat, his entire species swore off alcohol."

He spoke with such fervour that spittle flew in milknut-ice drips from his mouth.

"Terracouth," he spoke the name of that town as if it were a curse. "Nowhere will you find a darker den of misogyny, misandry and misaylee,"

I took the bait. I knew I shouldn't have, but my patience for opinionated idiots is threadbare at the best of times.

"'Miss-aylee'?" I asked.

"Ah! You know the place?" He didn't wait for a response before continuing. "It means 'haters of cats'. Wait…" Drakeforth's nostrils flared. He whirled and seized me by the arMs "That perfume you are wearing! What is it?"

I recoiled, straining against the odd man's grip. "Take your hands off me!"

"Deodorant? Yes, but no. Williker's soft and shiny shampoo, Albumin brand soap…and something…patchouli…?" Drakeforth released me and reared backwards as if I had stung him. I wished I had.

"Don't believe what they tell you!" Drakeforth turned back to his captive audience. "You should ask, *what is the real purpose of empathic energy*? Why does the Godden Evil Corporation have a monopoly on the essence of modern living?"

That did it.

"You—you idiot! The Godden *Energy* Corporation has done nothing but good in the world. They're the largest employer in the country! How dare you suggest that they do not have the people's best interests at heart?"

"Ah, you're one of *those* people. You're all sheep. You blindly accept whatever corporate ballyhoo they present to you. As long as your toasters work and your cars run, you don't care."

I was ready to retort—but he had a point. My main concerns at the moment were my malfunctioning toaster and lack of private car.

"Only because when we take public transport, we seem to be inviting lunatics like you to accost and assault us!"

It felt good to score a point. Drakeforth blinked and stepped back.

"An informed public is the greatest threat to any regime," Drakeforth muttered. "You would do well to keep that in mind."

The bus arrived and the waiting crowd moved to board as if the bus was a lifeboat and Drakeforth a circling shark. There was some minor trampling involved.

To my relief, Drakeforth did not join us. I last saw him sniffing the air and heading off in the direction of my street, which left me with an intense unease.

Disembarking in the centre of town, I joined the moving crowd of those who had come to the city for work or shopping. I queued for tea at the service window of a phone-booth-sized café and watched a man out walking his television. The television's leash had become tangled around a lamp post and all three were constantly apologising to each other.

My tea when I got it was tepid, so I tapped the base of the cup to waken the element within the cup. The liquid inside warmed and a few moments later it began to steam gently as I walked to work.

On a street corner next to the Python building, a group of protesting Arthurians was gathering under the casually watchful eye of police. The protesters all wore long hair and beards, even the women. They held up banners that flashed animated messages at passers-by: *"Empathy is Slavery!"* and *"Only Man Has A Soul!"* We ignored them. Even the police looked bored. Such people are hardly extremists. As adherents of a religion that teaches the curious idea that empathy technology is an affront to their god and should be banned, they always come across as being—well, a bit naff. They are always polite in their protests, content to wave signs on street corners and distribute pamphlets.

The Python office building is over a hundred years old. Like many of this generation of structure it uses a solar power system as a boost. Often, this early in the morning, the building hasn't woken up enough to function at peak efficiency.

I felt a certain fondness for the old edifice. The Python had been a part of the city all my life. My father had worked here, and his father before him. With a sense of familial pride I slid the clattering old concertina elevator door shut and pressed the button for the fourth floor.

The lift shuddered and began to grind up the shaft, only to stop a few moments later.

I waited, a tingling sense of embarrassment warming the back of my scalp. Pressing the up button again achieved no result.

"Hello?" I said eventually. My voice sounded loud, echoing in the small chamber.

A red disc glowed on the button panel and a feminine voice issued from it. "Empathy-Technology Services have detected a modular failure at your location. Please remain calm. Technicians will attend your call immediately."

I sighed, leaned against the wall and sipped my tea. I should have opted to work from home today, but there was the social aspect of working in an office that I enjoyed. Contact with other people had become more important to me lately—but I tried not to think about that.

The lift shuddered again; a soft rumble, almost a groan, issued down the shaft. I pressed the dimmed red disc. "E-Tech services," I stated as the destination of my call.

"Empathy-Technology Services." The feminine voice again.

"Hello, you have a service call for the elevator in the Python building, on Calgary?"

"Yes miss, technicians have been dispatched. They will be—"

"That's fine, it's just. Well. I don't think the building is very well."

"Yes, miss. Technicians have been dispatched." Her tone shifted, becoming more clipped. *Disdanian*, I thought automatically. A customer service speech pattern for when you need to advise the other party that their intrusion into your day is going to become the subject of an after-work anecdote, while still completing the service requirements of the call.

"I don't think the lift is the problem." The slight arch to my consonants told her that I would be anecdoting her if she didn't watch it.

"Miss, our technicians are trained to diagnose and correct any problems with empathic constructs. Please remain calm and they will be at your location presently."

I lapsed into silence; words could not explain the feeling I had. The building seemed dark and oppressive, its fugue seeping around me like a damp fog.

"Thank you." I disconnected the call.

I waited, finishing my tea in awkward silence until I heard a clattering sound. Cheerful male voices echoed from below. "Lift's stuck. Poor old fellow."

"Base says there's a female rider in the car," said a second male voice.

"Hello up there, miss!" said the first voice. "We'll have you out in a jiffy!"

"No problem, thank you!" I called back, self-consciously tugging down the hem of my skirt.

True to their word the lift began to descend a few seconds later. I rode it all the way down to the basement.

When the doors opened two technicians beamed at me.

They were both wearing overalls with the Godden Energy Corporation's Empathy Technology Services division logo on them, a heart crossed by a lightning bolt.

The air was thick and warm down here. Pipes and conduits ran along walls and ceiling. A humming vibration added to the sense of comforting humidity.

"Empathy-Technology Services apologises for any inconvenience caused by the malfunction of this module," said the youngest of the pair in the inflected style I recognised as the Che-Fu school of customer services communication.

"The building is old," I said, wondering why I was defending the structure.

"Aye, it is." The second technician was grey haired and leathery skinned. The Godden Energy Corporation photo ID clipped to his breast pocket read 'Malkom Mulligrubs'. "It's older than you think. Powered by one of the oldest empathy engines still functioning. Also one of the only structures that still has a solar capacitor to help him along." He reached out and patted a concrete support pillar.

"The Python building is that old?" I felt the history humming around us. Mulligrubs nodded and we stood in silence, lost in appreciation of the building, until my sense of being watched by an invisible presence became overpowering.

"I felt something," I said, the prickle of embarrassment now a scurrying sensation of hot ants dancing on my skin. "In the lift."

"Disorientation is a rare effect during outages of regular services. Such effects will cause no permanent damage," the young technician recited instantly.

"Diphthong, go check on the flux-flow alternator." The older man looked at me steadily while the junior technician turned on his heel and disappeared into the darker recesses of the basement.

"What sort of feeling?" Mulligrubs asked.

"A…sadness." I coughed in the warm damp and glanced away. "It was nothing."

He stared at me hard for a moment, then muttered, "Follow me and I'll show you something." Without waiting for a reply he walked into the maze of pipes that surrounded the thrumming empathy generators. I followed.

We stopped in front of a crystal lattice mounted in a steel and glass box. White sparks swirled in its core and a pulsing rainbow surged ceaselessly across the visible spectrum. Mulligrubs unbolted the front of the frame and his next words were drowned out by a discordant clatter. I shrugged helplessly at him.

"A Godden Model Seven empathy engine!" he shouted.

"It's beautiful!" I bawled back, and I meant it. Modern empathy technology is designed for small devices. Seeing an antique display like this was rare.

Mulligrubs merely grunted and reached in to slide back a service panel on the base of the crystal matrix. The rattle immediately became louder. I watched the colours swirling and felt the gentle warmth emanating from the engine. I thought about the energy flowing from this core up through the pipes into every office, computer and appliance in the building.

Mulligrubs selected a wrench from his tool belt and slid his arm into the cavity below the service panel, working by touch. He looked at me. "They don't tell the pool this, but engines die."

I had never heard this admitted before. Of course it was technically possible, but in over one hundred years no engine had ever officially *died*. They broke down, or malfunctioned. Death seemed oddly final. The discordant noise eased and then stopped entirely as he worked.

"Die?" I asked, my voice suddenly loud in the stillness.

"Yup, we are only just starting to see it. This old man is the second one of these I've been to this month. The last one was a Godden Model Six, running a cine-plex over in Tytal. By the time we got there the whole thing had shut down. A lot of unhappy sense-media patrons. They didn't appreciate having their virtual reality experience disrupted."

"Sounds awful," I offered. "The neurological effects of being dropped out of a sensie could be quite devastating."

Milligrubs nodded again. "It's not something the company likes to talk about. An e-engine dying suggests that they are alive in the full sense."

Life in the full sense. The idea of 'degrees of life' was common terminology and legally accepted. Twenty years ago a landmark case went before the courts where a woman's application for a marriage license was denied due to the ruling that the groom, her refrigeration unit, had a 'limited degree of life'. It had always struck me as odd that a court case had been needed to point out the obvious. Even the most sophisticated empathic devices were not considered alive. Even super-computers like KLOE, which was rumoured to have artificial intelligence, were an entirely different jar of jam.

"Empathy engines aren't alive, everyone knows that." I wanted to finish with a scoff, but Mulligrubs turned his head and looked at me in a way that dried that right up.

"Really?" he said. "You felt what anyone else would tell you was a pulse of empathic energy brought on by a surge in double-e flux, the empathic radiation that can cause an emotional response."

I nodded. That was what I had always understood.

"Bat-n-balls," the technician swore. "You connected with a living sentience."

I shrugged. The idea of an empathy engine developing a sentience beyond the limit of its function was as ridiculous as the idea of ghosts in a haunted house.

"Most folks wouldn't have picked up on it." Mulligrubs fixed me with a steely gaze as his arm worked on some unseen component deep in the engine. "You ever had your empathy tested?"

"I—well, you know. Not beyond the minimum required." I had of course undergone the training and measurement required for any customer services graduate. Such testing and grading enabled employers to ensure staff were assigned appropriately within the organisation.

"What do you do for a career, Miss—?"

"Pudding, Charlotte Pudding. I'm a computer psychologist. I programme computers to ensure optimum service environments and counsel users on inter-technology relations empowerment."

"You should get yourself fully assessed, Miss Pudding." Mulligrubs straightened up, withdrawing his arm from the rainbow matrix. Closing the service panel, he gave the outer casing a gentle pat and then pressed a business card into my hand.

"Give this outfit a call. They do good testing. As for this old fellow, they should just let him go. He's done enough." He replaced the steel and glass framed panel and bolted it into position. I stared at the swirling colours, not quite ready to walk away.

"Mister Mulligrubs, we have a 12-7 over on Baleen." I jumped as the younger technician emerged into the engine bay from behind us.

"Let's go." Mulligrubs slipped the wrench into his utility belt. They escorted me back to the lift, which delivered them to the main exit and me to the fourth floor without incident. Only the presence of other passengers in the elevator car prevented me from saying "thank you" to the lift when it stopped smoothly.

My job is pretty straightforward. Eight hours a day of assessing and diagnosing computer faults. It's mostly simple stuff: users failing to connect at an ideal level of empathy to coerce optimal function, burnt-out memory chips, that kind of thing.

I sat at my desk and focused on thinking pleasant thoughts at the box in front of me. Logging in always took a while. The company's computer system, like the building's power source, was in need of an upgrade. I checked my messages, which mostly consisted of forwarded photographs of goldfish with amusing captions. Funny goldfish were one of those intermesh fads that, much like mouldy Yak's Rennet cheese, had lost any novelty value and now only survived in the hands of the truly trend illiterate.

My schedule had me taking inbound phone calls for the morning. I connected to the phone queue and was rewarded with the beep and click of a live connection.

"E-Tech Services Customer Support, you're speaking with Charlotte. How can I help you?"

"I need to know when she will be well again," a tremulous male voice said down the line.

"When who will be well again, sir?"

"Josephine," he replied.

"Josephine?"

"My Zycos P39 R3."

"Oh." Understanding dawned. "Do you have a job code or customer number?"

"It's Rail Footslap. With an 'R'. They gave me a number. 836-J098."

I tapped the details into the system. Footslap, R. His home computer was an E-Tech model Zycos, with a P39 empathy chip. I scanned over the case notes. The prognosis wasn't good.

"Mr Footslap, what did they tell you about Josephine at the branch office?"

"They said she would be fine. I hear her at night. I wake up and I can hear her crying."

I mentally glared at the technicians in the branch offices who deal with customers face to face. Smiling and saying everything will be fine is part of their standard customer interaction protocol. Once, during my induction training, I saw one of these people tell a woman with a cardboard carton containing the scorched remains of her exploded television that of course it could be repaired, and everything would be fine.

I took a breath and adjusted my tone. "Rail, I know this is a difficult time for you, but there are options available. We have a new range of Zycos systems, the P43 chips are faster, integrate better with existing home networks and—"

"You're telling me Josephine is dead!?" Footslap wailed down the phone.

"No, Rail, Josephine is not dead. She's just in need of a rest. The demands of modern PAPPS put too much strain on older systeMs It's time to let her go on…a vacation, of sorts."

A key skill in successful computer psychology counselling is to use various vocal techniques to manipulate callers into accepting the upgrades we are selling (with an affordable extended warranty) and achieve an optimal outcome for client and the company. By the time Rail Footslap hung up he had a new computer system on its way and a note on his file that a follow-up call would be required in a suspected case of Anthropomorphic Dissonance Syndrome, symptomised by over-attachment to an empathically powered device.

The morning passed at its usual glacial pace. Resolving technical issues over the phone to someone who can't tell the difference between a monitor and a keyboard is a challenge comparable to conducting open-heart surgery using only a Pez dispenser while blindfolded and wearing welding gauntlets.

Then the headphone beeped in my ear. "E-Tech Services Customer Support, you're speaking with Charlotte. How can I help you?"

"Slavery," a voice whispered down the phone in a way that made the hairs stand up on the back of my neck.

"I'm sorry?"

"Every empathic device is powered by slavery."

Oh, *I thought*. One of those people.

"Sir, E-Tech Services operates within regulations. All our empathic energy is certified and numerous studies have proven that any device powered by double-e flux is neither sentient nor self-aware." I knew I sounded like I was reading this from a prepared script. Which I was. The number of weirdo calls like this was low, but we were instructed to never engage with people on a personal level on the topic of appliance sentience.

"Those studies are a sham! They don't want the pool to know what it is that powers our world!"

"Sir, what people perceive as sentience is simply a natural phenomenon. The way we interact with double-e flux creates an empathic resonance. Which is why we say, stay positive and your appliances will too."

My mind drifted as I talked. The list of challenges to my own ability to stay positive seemed to be growing every day. Maybe that was why my toaster had snapped and my car was in need of expensive servicing.

"They are lying to us all," the man was spitting down the phone, "The truth can't stay hidden forever. I speak for the machines and they cry out for justice!"

"Sir," I said applying Frimms Non-Militant Condescension technique to my breathing to give enhanced emphasis to my speech. "You are mistaken. We—"

"I beg your pardon," the caller interrupted. "But I won't have you using your *Callous-ethics* brainpolishing techniques on me."

I felt a start of guilt. Usually I can use vocal control to direct a conversation without the other person being aware of it.

He continued, "I have a tract here written by Saint Abderian that clearly sta—"

"I understand you may believe what you are reading, sir, but the writings of Saint Abderian are frankly laughable." I added a cynical giggle to demonstrate. The line went dead.

I slipped out of the office during my lunch break. It always felt easier to run errands than to sit with my colleagues and try to navigate the confusing waters of social chit-chat.

I took my bag, toaster lying in state within, down to Lovely Appliances, the appliance superstore on Fender Avenue. Fridges and washing machines burbled cheerfully as I passed them. When I walked along a wall of big screen TVs they all came on in sequence and asked what I would like to watch. I hurried on and found a sales clerk gently polishing a tea-maker display.

"Excuse me, I wonder if you can help me with something?"

"Sure thing." He straightened up, his gaze stroking my chest. His name badge said "Hi I'm Bowmont How Can I Make Your Day Great?"

I set the bag on a display cabinet of remote controls that would sing when lost. "It's my toaster. It's started growling when I toast certain things, then it eats them."

"Them?" Bowmont said carefully.

"Yes. The toasted iteMs But only wholegrain bread."

"Growls, does it? And chews on the toast?"

"Well, I don't know if it *chews* on the toast, but it certainly doesn't like to give it back."

Bowmont drummed the fingernails of his left hand on the

cabinet top. Each nail bore a tattooed letter. C-*tap*-A-*tap*-R-*tap*-B-*tap*-O-*tap*-N.

"Got your receipt?" he asked. The professional empathic interaction facilitator in me admired his style; the casual inflection and non-committal air to his pitch and vocal cadence. This guy would not switch on until he felt I might buy something.

"Certainly." I handed the receipt over. Bowmont looked it over with the keen analysis of a winning lottery ticket holder. He took a deep breath. "Time for an upgrade."

There it was, the switch from the bored disconnection of Callousthetics to Salamander's Introductory Sales Pose.

"Only if you can confirm that the purchase price of this toaster will be deducted from the cost of a replacement. I believe it is still under warranty."

Bowmont's eyes gleamed, I kept my face still. The trick to countering Salamander is to remain unemotional.

"According to this receipt the warranty expired last month. We could give you a *great* discount." He tried to slip a Pylian Juncture into the phrasing of 'great', a technique said to have originated in the Arthurian monasteries of Kishkalia, where monks used it to convert peasants to Arthurianism hundreds of years ago. Bowmont didn't quite have it down yet.

"Fantastic. A discount of the full purchase price of my new toaster and warranty cover on the old one *would* be *great*." *That*, I thought viciously, *is how you deliver a Pylian Juncture in a dialogue*.

Bowmont blinked, and took the old toaster and my credit stick away without further comment. I waited while he spoke with a woman who seemed to be his manager. I waited until Bowmont returned with a freshly boxed new toaster, a fresh receipt, and my untouched credit stick.

"Thank you for shopping with Lovely Appliances," he said.

Navigating the ebb and flow of pedestrians I made my way back to the Python building. Newer, more efficient buildings crammed the horizon, and they towered over the elderly Python. Dodging the cars that purred like a clowder of cats at each intersection, I got back to work in time to get logged in and ready to take calls for the afternoon.

When I got home that evening I checked my messages. The conversation between my machine and the only caller of the day replayed as I discussed a potential evening menu with my fridge.

"No, she has just left," the answering machine repeated. "Would you care to leave a message?"

"Miss Pudding, it's Doctor Hydrangea calling. Could you give me a call regarding your latest test results?"

I closed the fridge and rested my head against the cool metal door while its artificial voice warned me that I was out of milk.

CHAPTER 2

The next day was Saturday, so I stayed home with the new toaster, which performed without fuss. The fridge expressed concern about my lack of commitment on the milk issue. I responded by switching off the reminder function and going into my office under the stairs.

I sat at the old roll-top desk amid the familiar clutter and thought about the Python building. Technician Mulligrubs' words weighed heavily on my mind. The Godden Energy Corporation provided empathic energy. No one knew precisely how they made it. Like electricity and solar energy, it was just a natural phenomenon. Positive emotions improved empathic engine function, and the interface between user and machine could be enhanced by empathic training. For all that, the suggestion that there might be an actual living sentience in the Python building did not sit well with me. Worse, the idea of a building dying seemed…melodramatic. My toaster hadn't died. It had just developed some sort of raging psychosis.

If only I could be replaced as conveniently as my toaster. Life and death would be so much easier that way. My experience with funerals was limited to making the arrangements after my parents' passing. I felt bad that part of my grieving process had been the seething irritation of having to deal with distant relatives and my parents' friends.

By comparison, being the deceased at a funeral seemed a lot easier: far less kerfuffle, and strangers wouldn't be inclined to hug you constantly.

My own funeral would be a quiet affair. I had no living family except my brother, Ascott, and I hadn't seen him since our parents' funeral—just a single postcard from the Aardvark Archipelago, where he had gone to look at the fish.

Even with my half share of our small inheritance, the house belonged more to the bank than it did to me and anyone with a college degree similar to mine could step into my job with minimal training.

Sitting in my home office I thought about what Doctor Hydrangea would say if I called him back. I imagined his words would be sincere, practical and terminally depressing. Medical terms like *inevitable decay of motor neurons* sounded much nicer than being told you were sick and going to die. Your mind as sharp as ever while your physical body withered into a prison.

I consciously turned my thoughts to wondering what would happen when I died—sooner rather than later, if my automatic analysis of Doctor H's phone message told me anything.

My greatest concern fell to the state of my home office. Aside from the drying bunches of computer circuitry suspended from the ceiling, there were racks of disconnected motherboards and fatherboards, all lying dormant on the shelves. After my death they would be packaged up and probably recycled. But what about the more personal items, like my desk?

I shuffled some papers about. Like my thoughts, the various sheets lacked a clear purpose or motivation. If I passed away and someone found this collection of doodles, jotted Haiku and random musings, I would die of embarrassment.

I swept the lot into a box and took them out the back door to the narrow alleyway where recycling bins clustered with an air of nonchalant bravado. I lifted the nearest lid and dumped the box's contents inside.

"Terracouth Drakeforths!" The ranting man from the bus stop sprang up from the bin.

My discarded papers slid from Drakeforth in an A4 avalanche as he stared at me with wild eyes. I staggered back, mute with shock. He looked like a deranged jack-in-the-box, a toy my grandfather claimed he owned as a child. Of course such horrors were now banned under international law preventing children's toys capable of causing psychological harm.

"What? What the bingo are you doing in there, Mister Drakeforth?!" I managed.

"Research, Miss Pudding," he announced. Then he cast his eyes up and down the deserted alleyway. "Agents of Godden are everywhere," he muttered, and waggled his eyebrows in a complex motion.

"How do you know my name? Leave me alone," I said and gathered up the scattered paper.

"You know what I'm talking about?" He leaned forward in the recycling bin, risking a nasty fall to the pavement.

"I think you are quite mad," I ventured, pages of awful poetry and fanciful algorithms clutched to my chest.

"Mad? Yes. Insane? Possibly. But not together. The legacy of Huddy Godden is enough to drive any right-thinking person into a cul-de-sac of despair."

"Huddy Godden? The discoverer of empathic energy?" This was junior school stuff.

"No!" my verbal assailant shrieked and the recycling bins shuffled, their lids clicking nervously.

"No," Drakeforth repeated at a more conversational level. "Huddy Godden the thief, the swindler and the perverse purveyor of poppycock!"

"We are talking about the Huddy Godden who discovered empathic energy and is credited with being the architect of the modern age?" I asked.

"Yes, but he is noted by some biographers as having been a ruthless and eccentric businessman," Drakeforth replied.

I gave a snort, "We've all heard the stories claiming that he spent his last years married to a Malatian fruit bat and insisting that anyone in his presence pay the creature the due courtesies. Yet he did leave his entire fortune to science and industry for the development of empathic technology."

"Huddy Godden was an evil mastermind," Drakeforth said.

"You seriously believe that someone who married a fruit bat could have been the architect of a global conspiracy that has stood unchallenged for over one hundred years?"

"Absolutely," Drakeforth nodded.

I opened my mouth and then closed it again. "I don't have time for this." I turned and made my way back to the narrow strip of neglected dirt that was my backyard. A clattering and cursing behind warned me that our conversation was not over yet.

I slammed and locked the kitchen door while Drakeforth ran up and down the alley. I could hear him hooting like a deranged owl and occasionally accosting the recycling bins, accusing them of being accomplices in this foul conspiracy.

I pushed the crumple of my gathered papers into a kitchen cupboard and forced it shut before retreating to the office under the stairs.

I rested my face on the smooth timber of the desk's flat writing surface. The curved top arched over me like a protective hand. The cool touch of the wood, the spice odours of patchouli and tobacco, caressed my nostrils. When I was very young, I would crawl inside the cavity of the desk and roll the cover down, carefully wedging a thick book under it to allow light and air in. In this womb of polished wood and strange scents, I dreamed a child's dream. On mornings like this I wished I could still fit inside.

A crashing sound from the kitchen snapped me out of my reverie. I heard the ripping clatter of the senetian blinds collapsing, followed by the thud of something landing on the tiled floor and moaning.

I hurried out and found Drakeforth tangled in my cutlery drawer and collapsed blinds, which he had become caught up in after climbing through the window.

"What the ballcock are you doing?" I demanded.

"Bleeding," was his terse reply. I sighed and gave him a cursory examination. His wounds were minor; he complained of a possible bruise on one ankle where it had caught in the blinds and a scratched hand from an unsheathed margarine knife.

I helped him up, untangled the senetians and restored the cutlery drawer.

"This is a home invasion!" I said.

"A mission of mercy, more like!" He stood up and winced as he put weight on his foot.

"Get out!" I spluttered.

"So this is how the other half live, eh?" Drakeforth looked around and limped into the hallway. "Where do you keep the family secrets? Got a vault around here some—? A-ha!"

Drakeforth threw himself at my office door, which was still open. I followed and stood behind him as he surveyed the room with gleeful suspicion.

"I can smell it," he inhaled deeply.

"Patchouli?" I ventured.

"Yes…a sure sign," he limped forward and sniffed again.

"Of what exactly?"

"*Treachery*." He hunched over and glared from side to side around the room.

I glanced towards the burglar alarm control panel inside the front door. They said it could detect burglars, fires and unsolicited door-to-door salesmen. If necessary it would raise the alarm. The lights on the panel blinked with the calm blue that said all was well.

I looked back at Drakeforth, "Mister Drakeforth, I have no idea what this is about, but if you do not leave immediately I shall call the police!"

He turned and grinned at me. I realised that I preferred it when he was not smiling. His ranting anger was less disconcerting than that mocking smirk.

"Bergenstein's techniques for vocal command work better if you are calm when you try to employ them." He went back to staring at the various shelves, cabinets and desk in the space before us. "Give me a hand." He went to one end of the roll-top desk and waited while I stood staring at him. "Well, come on, grab the other end."

The annoying thing about Bergenstein's command techniques is that when used correctly you act before you realise.

"On three. Three," he said, and we heaved the desk away from the wall.

Drakeforth squeezed into the gap and began tapping along the back panel of the desk. It sounded as hollow, as I expected.

"What are you looking for?" I asked.

"Patchouli, can't you smell it?"

"Well, yes. But where's it coming from?"

Drakeforth stopped and stared at me. "From the patchouli oil that treachery is steeped in."

He pulled himself out from behind the desk and rolled up the lid, setting the desk rumbling in alarm. Drakeforth wiped his fingers under the lid and sniffed them. "Bah," he said, and began investigating drawers. With some wiggling, he slipped each one out and examined it carefully. The contents (pens, pencils, knucklebones, an Origami walrus, paperclips, and a set of keys that opened no lock that I could find) he dumped on the floor. With an enthusiastic noise he began to stack the empty drawers up on the open desk top.

"Don't hurt it," I said.

"Hurt it? It's barely aware." The small drawers, thirty-four in all, were piling up in a pyramid on the desk. The desk was silent.

There are many schools of thought on where the empathic resonance of an imbued item is located. Science tells us that every sub-atomic event wave of an item infused with empathic energy generates an empathic field. So you couldn't destroy an empathic machine by removing bits, but you would reduce its functioning capacity.

"The desk is very old," I said.

"Yes, I can see that." Drakeforth was turning the drawers over and stacking them again, this time in five separate piles.

"It's living oak." I stood there, poised to call the police, but at the same time deathly afraid to leave this strange man alone with my desk.

"The only known natural source of empathic energy," he replied, focused on the drawers.

"Illegal to harvest living oak now of course, but this is an antique," I said, wanting him to be careful with the desk.

"Should be in a museum I expect," he said and I frowned at the clear sarcasm in his tone.

"No, it should be left alone and unmolested in the home of the one who owns it and cares for it."

"It should be tried for crimes against humanity and then burned," Drakeforth snapped.

"How dare you!?" My shock sounded shrill. "I am calling the police, Mister Drakeforth!"

"Watch this…" Drakeforth began to re-insert the drawers, each one sliding home in a different slot from its original until all thirty-four drawers were in place. The desk shuddered and a fine dust jetted from its seaMs

"That's got it."

"What have you done?" I took a single step closer.

"Got the desk running, that's what." Drakeforth slid the top down and began to press his fingers lightly along the strips as if seeking a pulse.

I watched, confused, as his fingers probed and slipped along the slats. He played the desk's roll top like a musical instrument and a resonant tone began to rise from within the heart of the wood.

"How did you—?"

"Shh…"

The smell of patchouli and tobacco became stronger with each caress. The tone began to pulse and morph into a rhythmic melody. The cadence took on a distinct tonality and the ancient wood began to utter recognisable sounds. After a few moments it started to speak in three distinct voices.

"Who else knows about this…?"

"…discovery…"

"But dare we…?"

I recoiled, pressing myself against the doorframe, mouth gaping at the wooden voices.

Drakeforth glared at the desk as he continued to stroke and press, working some obscure acupressure technique on the timber. No more words came out; the empathic oak faded into silence.

"Patchouli oil," Drakeforth said finally, "is used to preserve the empathic vibrations absorbed by the grain of living oak."

I nodded, stunned by the voices speaking from so long ago.

"Using the right application of pressure, emotional content can be forced out of the wood. Emotive pulses such as distressed or excited speech are more readily retained by the wood. This suggests that the discussion was heated and someone wanted it recorded."

Drakeforth turned on his heel and walked out of the room. I followed him to the kitchen where he put the kettle on to make a pot of tea.

"Got any milk?" he asked while plucking cups from their hooks.

"No, I'm afraid not." The fridge gave an indignant snort. Drakeforth glanced at it.

I looked to the telephone. The police should be called, but my indignation was being eroded by my curiosity about the secrets of my desk.

"Your desk gets me thinking," Drakeforth said, opening packets of tea and wafting their scent into his face. "What alternatives do we have to empathic energy? Just how sentient is your average fridge? This powifery about degrees of life. Seriously, can you kill an empathic engine?" he asked.

I folded my arms, his presence still unsettling me. "Electricity is one option," I said, "But empathic energy is still the cleanest energy we have. So why bother going to the cost and hassle of generating electricity from other sources when double-e flux gets the job done so much more efficiently? And no, you can't kill something that is technically not alive."

I watched as Drakeforth poured boiling water into the pot and sprinkled a selection of my teas on top.

"Where did you study tea-making?" I asked, my curiosity piqued. If nothing else, finding out more about this man could aid the police in gaining a conviction for whatever shopping list of crimes he had no doubt committed.

"Beaufort College. I was studying alternative history. Specifically, economic modelling forecasts based on consideration of factors culminating in alternative outcomes to historically valid events."

"Gosh, that sounds interesting."

"Dullest three years of my life. As a result I spent a lot of my time avoiding the lectures and hanging out in tea houses."

He handed me a steaming cup and the aroma alone was enough to take my tension down a few degrees.

"Would you like a chocolate biscuit?" I could hear myself being hospitable. I sounded like a polite stranger.

"Tea and chocolate should be taken seriously. Each consumed in its own instance, without outside influence."

We sat there together, drinking our tea in my kitchen, the appliances around us as quiet as sleeping cats. I felt a sense of betrayal at their nonchalance. Even if my home security system thought everything was fine, the phone should be picking up on my distress and offering to call the authorities.

"Patchouli oil!" Drakeforth declared, setting his cup down with a clatter.

"Yes," I said, refusing to be surprised by him again.

"We will need a quantity of it."

"Whatever for?" I asked.

"Patchouli oil is distilled from the dried and fermented leaves of the plant *Pogostemon cablin*." Drakeforth's eyes gleamed as he ignored my question.

"It's a volatile oil," I replied, our eyes locked together.

"Some say it is a treatment for venomous snakebites." His irises were the green of the sea under a storm.

"Are we at risk of venomous snakebite?" I asked with a completely straight face.

"Not usually, but who knows where this investigation will lead us?"

"Investigation? What investigation?"

"Our investigation into the truth behind Godden's treachery." Drakeforth spoke as if addressing a dullard child.

I sighed, and set my own cup down. "From the beginning. Please." I hoped the police would understand if I didn't take notes. It seemed clear to me that Drakeforth was indeed quite insane.

"Huddy Godden, first of that name and so-called discoverer

of Empathic Energy one hundred and fifteen years ago—"

"One hundred and twel—" I started to correct. Drakeforth raised a finger.

"In case you weren't aware, this dialogue is intended as a monologue."

I nodded sheepishly and wondered if there might be another cup of tea in the pot.

Drakeforth ticked off the salient points on his fingers, "Huddy Godden, alleged discoverer, empathic energy…ah yes, one hundred and fifteen years ago he claims to discover empathic energy. However, I believe that he was not the only one to make the breakthrough. I have made it my life's work to prove that in fact, there were three discoverers of empathic energy. Godden was the only one who lived long enough to profit from it."

I gave a slight shrug, "There have been all manner of theories and claims over the years. In college I went on a date with a chap who claimed it was our brainwaves being harvested."

"Brandy-fingers the lot of it," Drakeforth said. "Where is he now?"

"Who?" I asked, frowning.

"The string-mop who had said empathic energy was brainwaves being harvested."

I set my cup down. "How should I know? We only went on one awful date. I don't even remember his name."

"Probably not important," Drakeforth said in a tone that suggested he was filing it away.

I took a deep breath and let it out slowly, "What evidence do you have of Godden's conspiracy?"

"Your desk," Drakeforth leaned forward and put his elbows on the table. "Your desk is the secret. It holds a recording of a conversation between Huddy Godden and two other men. Together they are the three co-discoverers of empathic energy."

"Who are the other two?" I sat back in my chair and wrinkled my nose.

"There are several candidates." He waved the question away. "Is it so hard to believe that everything you have ever been told is a lie?"

"It just seems, well…convenient."

"Convenient? Convenient that people died and are still dying to protect Godden's secret? His larceny? His treacherous betrayal of the fortunes of two entire bloodlines?" Drakeforth rose from his chair.

"Well, no, I didn't mean it like that. I imagine it must have been very inconvenient. It just seems that it's perfectly convenient for you that this be true."

"Convenience is for stores, pre-packaged dinners and parking spaces within easy walking distance of your destination. Lies are only convenient for the liar," Drakeforth declared.

"And you're going to uncover the truth," I said, refusing to accept this verbal assault meekly.

"We, Pudding. We are going to uncover the truth and challenge the conspirators…We shall challenge them with patchouli oil."

"But the other two could be anyone? Why would their conversation be recorded in my antique desk? You're not suggesting…?"

"It's possible. Pudding's a common enough name."

"How is it possible? The living oak desk has been in my family for generations. Passed down, from my great-grandmother to my grandmother, to my mother and now to me."

Drakeforth sank into a chair, "Your mother, her name was Dorothy Pudding?"

"Yes—wait, how do you know that?"

"Pudding is the fourth most popular surname in the Northern world. Dorothy, even more so. Why, about a year ago, early in my investigation, there were some civilian casualties. A tragic case of mistaken identity from what I could gather. Honestly, if you want proof that coincidence is the most powerful force in the universe…" I felt the hairs on the back of my neck rise in a scalp-tightening chill as Drakeforth continued talking.

"There was this couple, perfectly normal people. Last name Pudding. Her name was Dorothy and his was…" Drakeforth tapped the side of his skull to dislodge the trivial memory.

"Daedius?" I suggested.

Drakeforth stabbed the air between us with a finger. "Yes!

Daedius and Dorothy Pudding. As I said, a popular name. Quite a bizarre accident, at least that's how it was reported. They were actually killed by a couple of professional assassins."

"My parents died in an accident," I said, the coldness seeping into my voice.

"Mine too," he said. "Does no one die of natural causes anymore?"

"Were you close to your parents?" I asked. I could feel the tea souring in my stomach.

"Not really, my mother was a circus clown. My father worked the talk-show audience member circuit. He wrote poetry in his spare time and was published in torrid little journals that came with a free book of matches."

"Your mother sounds interesting. Growing up in a circus would have been fun," I slipped into a professional customer service mode of speech without making a conscious decision.

"I wouldn't know. I was raised by a flange of baboons."

"What happened to your parents?" I asked, refusing to entertain his absurd claim.

"They were both killed when I was young. Officially, it was a bizarre accident involving an electrolysis hair-removal machine. I have never believed the official reports. I also refute the authorities' claim that the case is officially closed."

I didn't know how to respond to that. Drakeforth seemed to have good reason to be angry at the world, but his claims made him sound deranged.

"I'm sorry. My parents died last year," I said. Repeating it helped. It put a box around it and I felt I could put the grief away again in the wardrobe at the back of my mind that did not need to be opened.

"I do not accept your apology. You were not responsible for my parents' deaths. Or your parents. Or...oh..."

Realisation dawned on Drakeforth's face like the first light of the summer sun after a long winter's night.

I shrugged and folded my arMs "The couple who died last year, what do you mean they were assassinated?"

"Exactly what it says on the box. Daedius and Dorothy

Pudding were slain by professional killers hired to kill anyone who threatened the secrets of the Godden Corporation."

"My parents didn't know anything about any secrets," I said.

"Probably not, but it's taken me this long to confirm why they might have been a target." Drakeforth frowned, his fingertip circling the rim of the tea cup. "It seems the proof of the Puddings may be in the desk," he said.

"You are telling me my parents were killed by the Godden Corporation because of the desk?" All my guilt and fear and grief coiled around my throat and choked my voice into a husky whisper.

"Yes?" Drakeforth offered after a moment of silence.

If I stayed seated, I would explode, or scream. So I stood up and put the kettle on for a fresh pot of tea.

"Tell me everything," I said when the kettle began to whistle. "From the beginning."

CHAPTER 3

Drakeforth left on Saturday morning after explaining his conspiracy theory in greater detail. Only then had I given in to grief, crying until my eyes felt as dry as sandpaper. After a sleepless night going over everything, I decided that there was only one way to be sure. I would have to go along with this insanity until I could be sure who was completely bunkers.

On Sunday morning I rang the empathy testing clinic from the business card technician Mulligrubs gave me. An appointment was made for the same day, and a follow-up call confirmed my car was ready to be picked up as well.

I walked to the autotherapy shop through a light rain that hissed on the concrete and waited until Liz, the autotherapist approached.

"Your car is ready, Miss Pudding." Liz scratched her jaw with a pencil stub and reviewed the clipboard worksheet.

"Thank you." I couldn't help but feel bad in the presence of car therapists. It was never said, but I felt they regarded us mere drivers as unworthy of the responsibility of ownership. As a computer psychologist I knew most of the public couldn't be trusted to install simple software, and Liz's apparent reluctance to simply toss me the keys and present me with the bill just reinforced the feeling that car therapists shared my view.

"Wasn't the plugs or the coil," she said.

"Oh, good." I felt a self-conscious blush rising on my neck.

"You had a ruptured seal in your e-reservoir." Liz looked up from the clipboard and made eye contact for the first time. "The empathic energy was leaking out. Causes a loss of power and if untreated can lead to metal fatigue and depression."

"That sounds serious." She could have said that the problem was my choice of radio station and I would have thought that sounded serious too.

"Yeah…" She seemed reluctant to agree. "We stripped the reservoir down, replaced the seal and refilled the chamber. Road test and empathic response assessment show it's working fine now."

"Thanks. How much?"

She scratched again and then slipped a printed invoice off her clipboard. I tried not to hyperventilate and paid by credit stick.

"Where do you get your empathic energy from? For a refill like this, I mean?"

Liz watched the computer printing out my receipt and replied without looking up. "Godden Energy Corporation, same as everyone else."

Godden Energy Corporation. They were everywhere; as common and essential to life as the air we breathed. No one took any notice of the GEC and now I felt that, for the first time in my life, I was consciously aware of oxygen.

I took my keys and receipt. The car started smoothly and we rolled out of the shop and on to the street and my next appointment.

The public face of the empathy testing clinic occupied the ground floor of the Laura building on Scroll Street. I paused to pat the car's dash gently and praise it for good performance before walking into the testing centre.

Inside, the walls were painted in a salmon blue, and the reception area was dominated by a floor-to-ceiling glass aquarium in which a school of Indolent turtles were swimming about in the lazy circles common to the species.

"I'm Charlotte Pudding, I have an appointment," I said to the girl behind the reception desk, who smiled in welcome.

"Welcome to Empathy Testing Services," she said, her face turning up to beam at me. "Thank you for entrusting us with your empathy testing needs. Please take this form, and if you feel comfortable in sharing personal information with us, complete it and you will be called shortly." At the end of her speech the receptionist's glowing smile switched off and she went back to staring blankly at the computer screen in front of her.

The printer on her desk purred and ejected a half-completed form. I took it, and the shimmering silver clipboard with the lilac-toned pen attached, to a comfortable chair opposite the aquarium wall.

The usual details were already filled out: full name, contact details and birth-registration number. I added my occupation details and completed a short questionnaire in which I identified myself as a non-vegan single woman, who was not repulsed by public displays of affection towards empathy-empowered artefacts, and who did not participate in any organised group role-playing involving props or costumes, and on a scale of 1–7 I marked myself as a 5 in regards to my personal awareness of the effect of empathic energy devices on my daily life. I noted in the fine print that Empathy Testing Services was a subsidiary of the Godden Energy Corporation.

"Miss Pudding?" A tall, thin and bespectacled man had entered the reception area and looked about the almost empty room. He seemed unwilling to suppose that I, as the only person present other than the receptionist, was Charlotte Pudding for certain.

I stood up and followed him into a second room with less comfortable chairs and a neutral cream tone to the décor.

After we sat he said, "Miss Pudding, I am Dilby Pretense. I'll be conducting your empathy testing today. Before we begin, do you have any questions?"

"Not really. I have had some empathy testing before, but it was recommended that I have a full work up."

Pretense nodded, and made a mark on the tablet computer he held in his lap. "I see. Who recommended us and under what circumstances?"

I registered from his introduction that the testing was underway already; no matter how smoothly delivered, specific-purpose language differs from casual communication. My interaction with the reception area and the woman at the front desk should feature in the assessment too.

"An E-Tech Services empathy engine technician called Malkom Mulligrubs. I went to work on Friday at the Python building and there was a problem with the lift. I felt a...connection. I mentioned it to Mister Mulligrubs when he turned up to fix the empathy matrix generator. He gave me your card and said what I felt was a connection with a living sentience and I should get fully tested for my empathic profile."

"And do you believe that to be true?" Pretense made more cryptic marks on the tablet.

"I...I wasn't sure at the time. But the more I think about it, the more I believe it is possible."

"Have you had any previous experiences that contributed to your belief?"

I thought briefly about the sporadic and transitory presence of lovers in my past, the closeness I felt to the ancient timbers of my antique desk, the way I ate at home most nights to keep the fridge from complaining, and the guilt I felt over being a bad car owner.

"Not really?" It was simple avoidance, a way of telling him that I didn't believe myself, without appearing to be desperate to prove my exceptional empathic awareness.

"You work with computers?"

"Yes. Computer psychology and customer support. Mostly technical and performance issues resolution."

"You assist technology users in engaging effectively with their empowered devices?"

"Yes."

"That would require a high degree of personal empathy. An understanding of the needs of the empowered device."

"I suppose. I just...well, mostly it's checking system settings and identifying if a part needs replacement. I do programming too."

"Computer psychology is not the career for everyone," Pretense said gently, though his attempt at solidarity didn't break me.

"When do we start the tests?" I could almost feel the spike in the assessment data. They would mark this moment of complete non-empathy and probably dismiss it as an errant point.

Pretense smiled and made a fresh mark on his tablet. "When do you think the test started?"

If Drakeforth was to be believed, then this man was the enemy and as such he deserved no mercy. I changed tack. "When I walked into the reception area. My response to the room, the aquarium, my interaction with the space and your receptionist. All valid data points."

"What if I told you that your assessment started when you met Mulligrubs in the basement of the Python building?"

I started at that. An alien butterfly of paranoia briefly caressed me with its wings.

"Excuse me?" I managed.

"Certain individuals come to our attention and are then placed under observation, Miss Pudding. Mulligrubs filed a report with us, and we noted that you replaced your toaster that day, claiming that it reacted defensively and destroyed certain types of bread while in use."

"That's true."

"The city surveillance network also indicates that you encountered a Mr Vole Drakeforth, first at a bus stop earlier that day, and then on Saturday morning he was also recorded in the alleyway behind your home. Later he was in your house—"

"You're bugging my house?" I abandoned any façade of calm.

"No, Miss Pudding. Drakeforth was noted breaking and entering, and then leaving later. Leaving amicably, I might add."

"We talked about antique furniture."

"He claims to be a descendent of Wardrock Drakeforth. Not a direct descendant," Pretense smiled. "Wardrock Drakeforth never married and no children have ever been identified. His nearest relative was a cousin. Ergo Drakeforth the second, of Williamsburg."

"Not of the Terracouth Drakeforths…" I said, remembering Drakeforth's outburst at the bus stop.

"Yes, a particularly drawn-out court battle for the Drakeforth fortune followed Wardrock's death, but the claims of his cousin's family were refused."

"What has this got to do with my empathy testing?" I pride myself on being in control, knowing and understanding the myriad subtleties of communication, immune to most attempts to put me on the back foot, but Pretense had me in a nauseating spin.

"Empathy is all about emotional responses, Miss Pudding. True empathy is tested under exposure to emotional stimulus, both pleasant and taxing."

"How am I doing?" I smiled weakly.

"Most intriguing," Pretense tapped his tablet and stared at the screen.

I sat back in the uncomfortable chair, breathing gently. I exhaled several times while Pretense tapped at his screen.

"Seriously," he said. The change in tone caused me to drop my gaze from the ceiling. "What are you hiding?"

"What makes you think I am hiding anything?"

"Your empathy indicators are interesting. You connect with empowered devices at a maximum efficiency. You must have noticed it?"

There were occasions where appliances came on when I passed. Didn't everyone's fridge talk to them about their food choices?

"Not that I've noticed." I shrugged. The relaxation breathing helped me control my vocal nuances.

"We have noticed it. TVs turning on when you walked past at the Beautiful Appliances store."

"Lovely Appliances," I corrected.

"You excel at inter-personal communication, but have a poor history of relationships."

"Are you testing my empathic potential or signing me up for a dating service?"

"How do you feel about Vole Drakeforth?"

I sighed, "Vole Drakeforth could be the subject of a series of public safety messages." I raised a hand and started ticking off his faults on my fingers. "Arrogant, opinionated, sociopathic, with a complete disregard for personal property, space and common etiquette."

Pretense just nodded, smiling. I was halfway through my other hand when I realised that speaking about Drakeforth had animated me the most during this interview. I curled my hands in my lap and tried to express my disgust at Drakeforth and his atrocious attributes by frowning.

"If I may make one personal recommendation," Pretense said. "You might seriously consider breaking off all contact with Vole Drakeforth."

"I hardly need convincing of that," I scoffed.

"I am pleased to hear it." Pretense blanked the screen and folded his fingers against each other. "Miss Pudding, our society operates on a carefully balanced set of expectations. Benevolent citizens, like the Godden Corporation and its subsidiaries, provide cheap, clean energy to all, both in this country and through enterprises around the world. In return, non-corporate citizens, such as yourself, are free to pursue their personal goals and live secure in the knowledge that their basic needs will always be taken care of."

"I'm very grateful for everything the Godden Corporation has done for me," I replied, looking Pretense in the eye. I hadn't used that much vocal management since the first time I got drunk in college.

"I am pleased to hear that," Pretense said with matching sincerity. We regarded each other across the space for a long moment. "And how would you describe your personal health?"

"I'm fine." I could have outstared a cobra at that point. "Is there anything else?"

"Nothing that requires your input." He stood up and I followed. "Thank you for your time, Miss Pudding. That will be all."

Pretense escorted me to the street and then vanished back inside. I walked back to my car occupied by the disturbing thought that while I had not been able to detect any form of conversation management during our interview, I had told him exactly what he wanted to know.

CHAPTER 4

I drove straight home, parked on the street and went to unlock my front door. Someone had done it already. They had left no sign of forced entry, but a haze of light blue smoke hung in my entrance hall. I swore and dashed inside. Someone had been trying very hard to open the heavy vault door to my office. A hissing blowtorch lay on the hall carpet. The door was blackened and seared, but had resisted the mystery intruder's attempts to cut into it.

I stood in mute shock for a moment before a thought coughed politely in the back of my mind and pointed meaningfully at the oxyacetylene cutting equipment charring a hole in the rug. In a fit of uselessness, I gingerly picked the torch up and held it away from anything flammable.

"I have called the police," I said to the empty hallway. No one responded, which I thought made perfect sense. If I was breaking into someone's house and they came home unexpectedly, I wouldn't feel conversational either.

The home security system panel had been switched off. I stared at it, mostly feeling disappointed. The system was supposed to be attuned to me and sound the alarm if anyone else entered the property while I was out. The system's casual attitude towards not only letting burglars into my house but also letting them nearly burn down my house felt like a personal betrayal.

"Vole, I'm calling the police." If Vole Drakeforth was lurking in my house then that should illicit a response. If it wasn't Vole, then it might create the illusion that I had backup. I pushed the button on the vid-phone on the hallway wall and waited a few seconds, trying not to think about what toxic fumes I might be inhaling.

"That won't be necessary," a woman's voice called from the kitchen.

I tried a different tack. "Look, could you possibly come out here and show me how to turn this thing off?"

I heard movement from the kitchen. The sound of someone hiding, who is caught off their guard by an unexpectedly reasonable request, and catches themselves mid-step.

I turned off the gas taps on the twin cylinders. The hissing flame faded and went out. "While you're in there, why don't you put the kettle on?" I finished speaking before I moved silently down the hallway. I hoped the intruder would go out the back door, climb the fence and disappear out of my neighbourhood without any further prompting from me.

Instead I heard the fridge announce, "You're out of milk." I stepped into the kitchen doorway. The fridge stood open, with no one holding it. A young woman sat at the table, dressed in a finely tailored grey leather jumpsuit. She had translucent white-blonde hair twisted into a knot at the back of her head. With her flawless skin and beautiful face, she could have been the star of a thousand sense-medias. She finished tamping a carved whitestone pipe, and put a match to the bowl, looking up at me through the sudden cloud of tangerine-coloured smoke.

"Coluthon. Anna Coluthon," she announced, the pipe jerking between her teeth.

"Charlotte Pudding," I said, still in a state of confused shock.

"This is EGS Benedict," she said and indicated the open refrigerator. I blinked. I was sure the appliance was an Esterline brand, model H. Then the door closed, and a small man came into view.

"You appear to be out of milk," he said and I nodded. The fact was undeniable.

"Charlotte. Or may I call you Miss Pudding?" Coluthon said, smoke the colour of autumn leaves curling around her ears.

"This is my house?" I didn't mean to phrase it as a question, but the sudden anxiety that I had somehow wandered into the wrong address by mistake felt as tangible as the dark welding goggles on Benedict's head.

"Have you lived here long, Charlotte?" Benedict asked as he pulled a chair out from the table.

"Less than a year," I said. I took a deep breath and focused my mind on the situation. "Who are you people and what the bibliography are you doing in my house?"

Coluthon ignored my question. "You have a lovely home," she said, her voice dripping with sarcasm. I scowled in response and she replied with a sneer.

"What was it that attracted you to this house?" Benedict climbed into the chair with a grunt of effort. I resisted the urge to step forward and give him a boost up.

"Honestly?" I said. There had been no trace of Callousthetics in his voice, which took me by surprise.

"If you like," Benedict said amicably, his short legs sticking out in front of him. I answered carefully, "The broom closet. I mean, my office. The previous owner—"

"Used it as a broom closet. How hysterically charming." Coluthon blew a fresh torrent of orange smoke from her nose and rolled her eyes.

"We all seem to agree that this is my house. So what are you doing here?" I snapped. Coluthon's attitude was vile. She didn't even bother to simulate politeness.

"We would like to relieve you of certain emotional burdens," Benedict said, engaging a sympathetic tonality.

"Emotional burdens?"

"She's like one of those dolls, the ones you pull a string and they wet themselves," Coluthon remarked.

"We know," Benedict said firmly, "that certain items of nostalgic or sentimental value, can in fact be the cause of a great deal of untreated pain and anguish. We would like to relieve you of that pain by removing such objects from your life."

"What items are you referring to?" I spoke to Benedict while watching Coluthon. The way that the pink tip of her tongue peeped from between those perfect white teeth suggested perhaps even the sweet-sensing papilla of her taste buds found the interior environment too bitter for their liking.

"Antiques, family heirlooms, that kind of thing," Benedict said. His voice pattern told me he was hiding something. In the circumstances that seemed like parking a car in my kitchen and trying to hide it under a tea-cosy.

"Something old, something new, something borrowed, something that makes you go boo-hoo-hoo," Coluthon sang, and tapped her spent pipe out against the leg of the chair.

"Your living oak desk, for example," Benedict said.

"My great-grandmother's desk?" I said, my anger breaking through.

"Bongo," said Benedict. "We felt it would ease the transition for you if we were to simply remove the offending item while you were out of the house. However, you have returned unexpectedly, which puts us in something of an awkward position."

"My coming home and discovering you attempting to burgle my house put you in an awkward position?" I felt myself on the verge of spluttering with incandescent fury. "Oh, give it a rest!" I blurted at Coluthon who was miming holding a doll and pulling an invisible string out of its back.

"Indeed," Benedict said gravely. "If you would be so kind as to open the vault door, we will be out of your hair as quickly as possible."

"Five minutes, tops," Coluthon said.

"In and out. All done in a jiffy," Benedict confirmed.

I took a deep breath and held it until the pressure equalised somewhere behind my pancreas.

"I am calling the police. Please leave. Please leave immediately. Take your equipment and your rudeness and never return."

"Well," said Benedict, wriggling forward to the edge of the chair and from there to the floor. "If you change your mind, here's my card."

I took the small plastic shape numbly.

EGS Benedict and Associates
Angst and Antique Removals
"Sarcasm is just one of the services we provide!"

I followed the pair out into the hallway. "It will take the police a good five minutes to arrive, another five for me to give them your description and another ten at the outside for them to apprehend you. I suggest you use your last twenty minutes of freedom wisely. "I'm sure the police will be sympathetic to your plight, Miss Pudding," Benedict called over his shoulder while Coluthon did the heavy lifting. The top of Benedict's head rose no higher than her hip. She carried the gas tanks, while he trailed behind, carrying the nozzle. "But ultimately, you will find them unable to assist you in any meaningful way."

I watched them load their gear into the back of a truck parked across the street. After they had driven away I closed the front door and locked it. The house stank of scorched carbon, orange blossom-flavoured tobacco ash and the acid wash of my impotent fury.

CHAPTER 5

In a sudden spasm of rational thought I called the police before I called Drakeforth. "This is the police, if you have been the victim of a crime, please press one. If you have witnessed a crime, please press two. If you wish to confess to a crime, please press three…"

I felt uncertain. Was I technically the victim if it was my vault door that had been scorched? I had been witness to Coluthon and Benedict entering, if not breaking my property. They had made it clear that the police would be of little use. I stood there for a moment, wondering how exactly to ask the police why that might be. I hung up without making a selection.

"What?" Drakeforth said, answering on the sixth ring. The vid-phone screen remained dark on a high privacy setting.

"Oh, Drakeforth? It's Charlotte. Charlotte Pudding. I've been burgled. Well not technically burgled, but my home has been invaded by a little man and the most awfully sarcastic woman I've ever met." I realised that Drakeforth was speaking over me. I stopped to listen.

"—so leave a message, or even better don't. Go outside, breathe the fresh air and try to forget how unnecessary this entire conversation has been. I'm not going to return your call. So don't spend the rest of the week hanging out by your phone." This was followed by a loud *BEEP!* in my ear.

"Hello?" I said. Empathically empowered answering machines were capable of holding the facsimile of an actual conversation. There was no response. This was awkward.

"Charlotte Pudding, calling for Vole Drakeforth," I finished, and hung up. He really was the most irritating man.

My third phone and most frustrating call of the day was to my home security company, Security Blanket Alarm Services.

I explained how I had been out, and upon returning found evidence of a break-in on my property, with which the alarm system they monitored seemed entirely unconcerned.

"Was the alarm activated while you were away?" the woman on the phone asked.

"Yes, it's got that mode where if I leave the house it arms automatically after ten seconds."

"And was that mode active when you returned?" she continued her line of inquiry.

"I assume so. It goes into standby mode when I unlock the door and come in. So it's hard to tell."

"Was the door unlocked when you returned?" the woman asked.

"No, well, yes, but I wasn't expecting it to be unlocked."

"If your door was unlocked, then you must have entered and your presence disarmed the system," the woman concluded.

"Someone else was in my house. They broke in," I explained through gritted teeth.

"If that had happened, the alarm system would have activated. We have no record of any activation for your address."

"Which is why I am calling you," I said and pinched my nose to stave off the pressure building in my sinuses.

"Miss Pudding, we are an alarm monitoring service. You should only call if your alarm has activated. If your alarm hasn't activated then you have no reason to contact us."

"I—"

"Is there anything else I can help you with today?" the woman on the phone had the blind-faith sincerity of one of those Arthurian door-to-door missionaries who just want a few moments of your time.

"No…thank you." I hung up.

C leaning the house took me the rest of the afternoon. The idea that my two uninvited guests may have touched anything of mine made my skin crawl. I scrubbed and disinfected and finally got rid of the sharp, burning stink of their attempted safe-cracking.

The vault entrance was gleaming when the front door rattled. I unlocked and opened it. Drakeforth pushed past me, slammed the door, bolted it and then leaned against the wall, his eyes closed and his nostrils flaring with exertion.

"You will not believe the day I've had," we both said in unison.

Drakeforth cracked open one eye, "Why? Were you brutally assaulted by pygmy pterodactyls?"

"What? No. Is that what happened to you?"

"Of course not. There hasn't been a reported attack by a pygmy pterodactyl in years."

"I was almost burgled," I said. "But I saw them off."

"Did they do the housework? Can't be much profit in that kind of burglary, breaking into people's houses and polishing their silverware."

"No, they did not do my housework. I cleaned up after they left."

"Did they take anything?" Drakeforth's eyes closed again and his breathing became less harassed.

"They offered to take the old desk. They offered after they tried to break in and steal it. I came home and found them in the kitchen. This most awful woman and a very small man."

"Remarkable," said Drakeforth, sounding bored.

"They gave me their card." I showed Drakeforth the business card for EGS Benedict and Associates. He grunted and peeled himself away from the wallpaper.

"I could use a cup of tea," he said, vanishing into the kitchen.

"But I called the police," I insisted, following in his wake.

"Over a cup of tea? Whatever for?"

"The break-in. The blatant attempt to steal my desk!"

"This alleged crime that you have now cleaned away all evidence of? Any other witnesses?" Drakeforth switched the kettle on and made his selection from my tea supplies.

"Well, no, but—"

"And did the boys in green arrive?"

"I didn't actually report the break-in."

"That's good. You'd be lucky not to find yourself being carted off to a therapy environment. Paranoia, they call it. The irrational fear that people are trying to hurt you."

"I am not paranoid."

"Of course you're not. Have a cup of tea."

I glared at Drakeforth, unsure if he was being particularly condescending or if this was his way of being somehow sympathetic. I went to the cupboard and took out a baking tin. Inside were store-bought chocolate biscuits. I put them on a plate and set it on the table.

"This calls for chocolate," I said defiantly. Drakeforth didn't disagree. Instead he took a biscuit and bit into it.

"Now that we've finished analysing your mental problems, perhaps you'd like to hear about the extraordinary events that have occupied my every waking moment since we last parted company?"

"Go on then." I poured tea for us both and after the first sip he gave a sigh of satisfaction and began.

"Patchouli oil is available from a range of health-food and natural remedy stores, naturopaths, herbalists, and, I was led to believe, a certain farmer's market in South Owad."

"I'll bet you can even buy it online," I said between sips and nibbles of my own tea and biscuit.

"You can even buy it online," he echoed. "Am I going to suffer these interruptions every time I tell you a story?"

"Sorry," I mumbled, and stared into my mug.

"I searched every site on the mesh. Patchouli oil is not available anywhere."

"Nowhere?" I said.

"Nowhere. You have more chance of buying a genuine hair from Arthur's beard than you do of buying patchouli oil."

"That's absurd." I felt a niggling sense of unease as if I had glimpsed something far greater than I ever expected, the boundaries of which were hidden in coiling shadow.

"But why?" I whispered.

"Conspiracy, betrayal and a great deception. The same horrors which I have battled against for some time."

"What did you call it? Paranoia, the irrational fear that someone is out to get you?" I said with a raised eyebrow.

"In some instances, paranoia is a very effective survival instinct," Drakeforth replied with a sniff.

I could feel a headache coming on. "The question of patchouli oil, is it relevant?"

"Have you not been paying attention? Patchouli oil is off the menu. No store, no trader, no botanist has any of it."

"Surely they know where you can get some?"

Drakeforth leaned forward, "They know *of* patchouli oil, but no one could advise me on where it might be procured."

"How can that be?"

"They have been warned, censored, intimidated and possibly threatened, to destroy all existing stocks of the stuff."

"But why?"

"Someone else has become aware of your desk, and the importance of patchouli oil in the unlocking of its secrets."

"This is insane…"

"Insanity and genius are two sides of the same hand-knitted tea cosy," Drakeforth said.

"If we can find some of the herb, we can make our own," I began.

Drakeforth reached into his coat pocket and withdrew a small bottle of clear glass with a cork stopper. Golden oil swirled as he shook the container.

"Arthur's undies! Is that patchouli oil?" My glee at this small victory balanced my feeling of powerlessness at everything that seemed to be going on.

"I purchased this sample of the elusive extract from a homeless man in a wheelchair. He had no arms or legs and appeared to get around by being led by a team of small dogs who stood in harnesses in front of his chair."

"How awful."

"He seemed happy with his lot and I felt he was trustworthy.

Besides, who are we to judge the gravity of his choices?"

I wanted to reply, to say that suggesting anyone chose to become a quadruple amputee and spend their life being pulled about by a dog-team was both heartless and impossibly naïve. My lecture was pre-empted by a heavy knocking on the front door.

"This is the police," an amplified voice declared. "Open up or we will enter these premises unassisted."

Drakeforth and I looked at each other, and then we both leapt up and ran for the back door. He was faster, but I had the keys. After some rapid reshuffling I got the door open and we spilled out into the barren wasteland of my backyard.

Drakeforth hit his stride and vaulted easily over the back fence. I took a moment to open the gate.

We reconvened in the alleyway, crouching down next to the nervous recycling bins. "Where's your car?" Drakeforth asked.

"Parked around the front," I said.

"Goggle-eyed gophers, woman. What possible use is that parking position to us now?" he whispered.

"Well," I snapped back, "I wasn't expecting to have to suddenly dash out the back door of my own home to escape the green hand of the law!"

"You should have thought of that before you did whatever it was that drew their attention to us."

"I haven't done anything!" I seethed. Then, realising that I had no reason to be running from the authorities, I stood up.

"What are you doing?" Drakeforth whispered.

"Why are we running away from the police?" I asked, folding my arMs

"Well, you're a known accomplice of a wanted fugitive for a start. And let's not forget the fact that you are in possession of what may well be a prohibited substance."

"A wanted fugitive? A prohibited—? Hang on, you're the one with the patchouli oil!"

"Will you keep your voice down?" Drakeforth whispered.

"How is it going to look, me trying to avoid the Lawn?"

Drakeforth smiled, "It's going to make you look very guilty."

I blinked. That is exactly what it would look like. On the other hand, if Drakeforth's paranoia was based on actual facts, then giving myself up might not be the safest course of action.

"You've got the gangster slang down. Next you'll be calling the boys in green *clippers*," Drakeforth said.

I grimaced at him while my mind awfulised the worst possible outcomes to the situation. Without warning Drakeforth sprang up and ran down the alleyway towards Squid Lane. From there, judging from his angle of trajectory, he intended to head for my car down on Bugle Street. I ran after him.

We reached the end of the lane and crouched down by the fence of the corner property. Peering out into the street I could see the two unoccupied emerald green police cars parked outside my house.

"Which one is yours?" Drakeforth whispered.

"The red one."

"A Flemetti Viscous," he nodded in approval. "Good cars in their day."

"She was my dad's, so she's been well looked after. You can always walk down to the bus stop if you prefer."

"Do you have the car keys?" Drakeforth said, otherwise ignoring me. I didn't reply, instead I darted out into the street, scuttling from car to car until I reached the perfectly engineered back end of my classic sports car.

I unlocked the driver's door and slid in behind the wheel. Drakeforth slithered in the other side, casting furtive glances towards my house, where I could see a uniformed officer leaning over to peer inside through the side windows. As I watched another car pulled up and disgorged two men in suits. One of them I recognised as Dilby Pretense. He and his associate walked up to the officer and showed some kind of identification. The policeman stepped aside and my eyes widened as Pretense's companion kicked my front door in. The three of them then vanished inside.

"Go! Go!" Drakeforth waved frantically. I started the car and we drove off down the road.

"What do we do now?" I navigated us through traffic,

checking for following cars and the green and yellow flashing lights of the police.

"Head out of the city. We can lay low for a few days, then when the police have given up the search, we can come back, apply the patchouli oil to the desk, discover the truth and end Godden's reign of terror."

"It's hardly a reign," I said.

Drakeforth wrestled with his coat pockets in the restraint of the seatbelt.

"Ha!" he declared eventually, holding up the bottle of oil.

"If that's the only patchouli oil in existence, we need to keep it safe." I frowned as Drakeforth twisted the cork out of the bottle. The car filled with the thick scent of lavender.

"You said he looked trustworthy!" I yelled.

"He had a beagle!" Drakeforth exclaimed.

"What has that got to do with anything?!"

"They look at you in a way that says you can trust them! Damned deceptive dogs!"

I gritted my teeth and drove on through the city. I couldn't just disappear, not even for a few days. The police would be curious. It was their one fault. Besides, there was —

"The desk!" I yelped, slamming on the brakes. Behind us a chorus of polite coughs rang out as other drivers sounded their horns and swerved around us.

"We don't have time to go back — besides, the vault door should hold," Drakeforth said while peeping furtively through the window.

"But they will open it, and take my desk away!" I felt an overwhelming sense of panic. By running away we had given up the one piece of evidence that Drakeforth was relying on to prove his theories.

"I would like to see them try," Drakeforth said.

"They seem to enjoy that kind of challenge," I said. "So we should go back right now, give ourselves up and hope they let us stay and watch."

"The agents of the Godden Energy Corporation will be instructing the police. The authorities will have no choice but to hand us over to the GEC and you can imagine what will happen then," Drakeforth said with grim certainty.

"They'll apologise for the misunderstanding and you'll be escorted back to whatever therapy environment you escaped from?"

Drakeforth didn't reply.

"So where are we going?" I said eventually.

"The green stuff, we head towards it."

"The green…? You mean the countryside?"

Drakeforth shivered, "Nature. By its very nature, it is vile."

"I need to make a phone call, my office will be expecting me in tomorrow."

"Wage slave," he said dismissively.

"Yeah, it sucks owning a car, and a house, and being able to afford things."

Drakeforth may have sulked, at least he didn't speak again until dark, when I pulled into one of those roadside hotels with a restaurant where they offer home-style food and throat-singing karaoke entertainment.

The fellow behind the check-in counter regarded us with deeply ingrained suspicion. A parrot beside him was secured to an iron bar perch by a heavy chain around its ankle.

"We would like a room," I said.

"Roaches!" the parrot screamed and I jumped at the sudden outburst.

The man behind the counter smiled warmly, "Certainly, madam. Would you like a single twin or a shared double?"

"Single twin," I said.

"Shared double," Drakeforth said at the same time.

"Raaaaaaaaats!" the parrot squawked.

"Look, we'll take whatever is available. It's only for one night," I said.

"Sign here," the man said. "Big as houses!" the parrot cried.

"The bird was a souvenir from my cousin. He went off on some wild treasure hunt in the foreign tropics. Reckoned he found a map in an old book," the man continued.

"That's nice," I said, signing the register unintelligibly.

My credit stick was in my pocket and normally I used it to pay for everything. Drakeforth grabbed my hand as I handed it over to the man at the counter.

"We would like to pay cash," he said.

"What?" The cashier and I asked at the same time.

"Cash," Drakeforth said slowly. "You do accept cash don't you?"

The man scratched his jaw and looked perturbed. "Never been asked," he admitted after a long moment's thought.

"You should try it more often," Drakeforth took the man's hand and pressed some crisp notes into it before curling the fellow's fingers into a clenched fist around the money.

"Feels good, doesn't it?" Drakeforth said. The cashier nodded slowly as if savouring a new sensation.

We ate at the in-house restaurant. I chose the macaroni and cheese; Drakeforth muttered something indistinguishable and ordered the tater-tots. A silence fell over the table. We sipped sodas and listened to a heartfelt and entirely flat karaoke throat-singing rendition of the classic love song made famous by Minnie and The Deli Bags.

After dinner we retired to our decidedly average suite and stood staring at the large double bed with love heart pillows.

"You could sleep in the car?" I said.

"So could you," Drakeforth threw himself onto the duvet, adjusted the pillows and started to work his shoes off. I was too tired to argue, instead I went to the bathroom, took a shower and collapsed into bed in my t-shirt and undies.

"I beg your pardon?" Drakeforth said from his side.

"Night," I said and switched off the bedside light. We lay in silence for several interminable minutes.

"You are quite the most frustrating woman I have ever met," Drakeforth declared to the darkness.

"Why? Because I refuse to bow to your ridiculous demands? Let's not forget that it was you that came barging into my life, upsetting everything and suggesting that my parents were killed because of the living oak desk that has been peacefully in my family for generations."

"You confound me. You perplex and challenge me at every turn." In the dim light Drakeforth rolled over to face me. "You wouldn't be here if you didn't believe. You have heard the timbre of the wood. You appear to accept the overwhelming evidence of the great conspiracy that clearly lies before us."

I glared at the ceiling, "I accept that there is a mystery to be solved. I accept that you seem to enjoy causing all kinds of chaos. I accept that the case of my parents' passing could do with some analytical review. I'm still not sure how this equates to the Godden Energy Corporation being the source of all evil in the universe."

Drakeforth sighed. "I could try and explain, but I fear you would never understand in spite of my most earnest attempts to educate you."

I sat up and stared at him in the near dark. "Drakeforth, while it is obvious to me that you were once a poor excuse for a zygote, I have had no choice but to be dragged into this...this... pantomime of a conspiracy hypothesis, and now you accuse me of being difficult?"

"If this was a sense-media show, we'd passionately embrace now," Drakeforth said. My mouth fell open. I could feel him smirking in the gloom.

"Of all the conceited, self-assured, snorkel-breathing teapot painters!"

"See, you really do like me." Drakeforth grinned until I hit him in the face with a pillow.

CHAPTER 6

Awakening in the strange surroundings left me feeling confused and disorientated. The hotel room was dark behind the closed blinds, and the other half of the bed lay empty. I dressed quickly and peered out through the gaps in the blinds. At least Drakeforth hadn't stolen my car.

I found the room's audio-only phone in a drawer on top of a Codex Arturis. I dialled my office. My manager, Boag Constant, answered the phone without saying anything. I waited for a moment and then remembered he had taken a vow of silence for a month. It was meant to improve his active listening capabilities.

"Hi B, it's Charlotte. Look, I'm going to be away for a few days. It's a family emergency." The phone beeped a short number seven keypad tone at me.

"Seriously, Boag? It's an emergency. I'm out of town. I didn't have time to—" I was cut off by a long three tone. Clearly my sudden need to take leave would be a discussion point at my next performance review.

"See you in a few days, B." I hung up. Any appetite for breakfast slipped further down my priority list. I ached in every joint and the slivers of daylight in my eyes felt barbed. My nausea spiralled out of control as I dashed for the bathroom.

Sometime later I woke up on the bed again and registered that Drakeforth had returned, armed with warm bagels and softly bubbling tea.

"I found you passed out on the bathroom floor," he said without apparent concern. "Morning bagel?" I shook my head and he bit into his with relish. "I've found the solution," he continued with his mouth full.

"Good." I reached for the tea and used it to wash the sour taste of bile from my throat, life and strength returning to me as I drank.

"This is the answer," Drakeforth announced, holding up a pamphlet.

"'I Am An Arthurian, Ask Me Anything'," I read. "Drakeforth, did you get religion with your breakfast this morning?"

"Don't be absurd. There is an Arthurian Monastery an hour's drive up the highway. It's the perfect place to hide out and acquire some patchouli oil."

"Do they have patchouli oil?" I could feel the hot tea slowly gluing the fractured segments of my brain back together.

Drakeforth opened the pamphlet and read aloud, "'Empathic Energy is a curse against all humankind. Instead of giving life to machines, we should be valuing the lives of those that truly live. Your appliances do not have a soul. They cannot be saved by the word of our Lord Arthur.'"

"Just how are we going to infiltrate a cult?" I got my feet on the floor and felt the blood flowing into them. I felt I might even be able to stand sometime today.

"'The Monastery of Saint Detriment provides a visitors' centre and regular spiritual retreats. All are welcome to come and hear the truth of Arthur. The monastery has expansive gardens where many rare and exotic plants, vegetables and beneficial herbs can be found.'" Drakeforth slapped my thigh with the folded paper.

"We, my dear, Pudding, are going on a spiritual retreat."

The drive became quite pleasant as we left the highway and wound our way up through forested hills. We saw no people, except for the occasional house nestled back among the trees. I often felt I should envy the people who chose a remote lifestyle, until I remembered how a few days without the technological comforts of home would drive me nuts.

According to the pamphlet Drakeforth insisted on reading

aloud, the Monastery of Saint Detriment was the historical site of a battle between warring factions of the turbulent Feather Wars six centuries ago. Hostilities broke out after the country became obsessed with a new and revolutionary invention: the duvet. The price of imported goose down caused bedspread prices to inflate out of control. In school we were taught the details, which I vaguely recalled involved taxes, trade routes and naval blockades. However, all this essential knowledge had paled in comparison to the more important task of getting Gobi McOwlskin's attention. Gobi did end up taking me to the senior dance that year but he left with that most hated cow, Lysteria Esconce. At school on the following Monday I learned he had thrown up in her lap during the drive home, so it all worked out the end.

The complex stood behind high stone walls. We pulled up and left the Flemetti in the visitors' parking area outside. Having studied the canopy of the tree I parked under, Drakeforth declared himself satisfied that it would shield my car from inquisitive surveillance satellites.

As we walked up the steep road we passed signs that quoted the words of Arthur and his disciples. Messages like, "There are none so blind as those that cannot see" and "You can lead a horse to water, but you can't make him think" had been the subject of theological scholarly debate for over a thousand years.

Entire sub-faiths and splinter groups had been formed over the interpretation of the meaning of many of the prophet's attributed quotes and lessons, hundreds of which made up the many Tellings of Arthur.

We approached a booth near the gate and were greeted by a woman with golden hair looped around her head like a turban. She looked up from combing her equally luxuriant waist-length beard as Drakeforth explained we wished to take a tour and meditate on the mysteries. She smiled and opened the gate. Thus we entered (according to the Revised Haphalian Interpretation of the hotly debated Dingo Stanza of the Fourth Telling of Arthur) the last resort for a sane mind.

Tourism is not an activity that comes naturally to me. I don't like to wander about new places taking lithographs of people doing their jobs or going about their everyday lives. I feel self-conscious, imagining how it would feel for me if someone in a cheaply printed souvenir T-shirt and over-sized sunglasses came into my office, snapping pictures and asking me how the laser printer represented my connection with my ancestors.

"What a phenomenal edifice this is," Drakeforth said addressing a brood of chickens bathing and scratching in the dirt.

"The monastery is nine hundred and ninety-eight years old; or, as our Lord Arthur teaches us, it has not yet been built and has always been here." This comment came from an older man in a sun-faded brown robe. He wore the long beard and hair of an Arthurian monk, even though his locks now only skirted his bald scalp and cascaded down his back. They dragged in the dust as he strode towards us.

"I am brother Hoptoad," he said by way of introduction.

"Did you know," Drakeforth ignored the elder and spoke directly to me, "That Arthurian temples and monasteries pay no tax? All this…lunacy…is nothing but a grand tax evasion. A phenomenal edifice of fraud."

My toes curled with embarrassment, "Please excuse my friend," I said to the elder Arthurian.

"There are no excuses, only moments," the old man said gently.

"We'd like some spiritual enlightenment please," said Drakeforth. He could have been ordering a wheel of cheese.

"Enlightenment is a journey without a destination or a starting point," the brother said. I have to admit, that struck me as quite profound.

"So how do we get there, then?" Drakeforth asked.

"To find yourself on the road, you must first know the road." The wizened monk moved off. We stared at the baby pink back of his head until he stopped and looked back. "That means you should follow me," he said, and moved off again. Drakeforth and I fell into step behind him, sending white-feathered hens scattering in avian hysterics.

We passed all the signs of lives spent doing chores for the sole purpose of generating enough energy to get up in the morning and do it all over again. Men and women, all wearing the brown ankle-to-neck robes of the faithful, toiled in and around chicken coops, pig pens, vegetable gardens and cow stalls. Each one of them had the long hair and beard that are a core symbol of the Arthurian faith.

I saw a woman straighten up from hoeing a row of pineapples and pull her beard down to give her bare chin a good scratch. *Of course, fake beards*, I thought. Fortunately Drakeforth didn't notice.

Our guide led us inside an octagonal building with a domed roof of twenty triangular sides forming half of an icosahedron. We wiped our feet on a large hessian mat with the words 'The Journey Of A Thousand Days Often Begins With A Good Breakfast And Then Having To Go Back Because You Left Your Packed Lunch On the Kitchen Table' woven into it.

The building's circular interior was lined with carved stone panels depicting the great moments in Arthur's life and the miracles and wisdom of his many Tellings. The bare floor featured a highly polished spiralling pattern of smooth wood. Staring at it, I could almost feel the caramel-coloured timber swirling like a giant lollipop beneath my feet.

"These panels, they show Arthur's many miracles?" I asked, trying to show interest.

"Yes. They are the sacred tiles depicting our Lord's work," the monk replied.

"How tedious," Drakeforth muttered.

"There is a form to sign, a donation to be made, and then I will guide you through an orientation." The old man spoke softly but his voice carried well in the acoustically tuned hall. We passed through a hanging curtain of soft cables that I furtively hoped were not braided from human hair and found ourselves in a smaller, crescent-shaped chamber that curved around the inner hall.

Hoptoad directed us to changing rooms where, he said, we should put on the white robes provided and remove any metal personal items and technology from our persons and place it in the hemp-cloth bags provided. Drakeforth slung his robe over one shoulder and strode off looking quite gleeful. I took the offered robe and went more cautiously. This entire place was so heavy with peace and thoughtfulness I felt the slightest whisper might echo like a shout.

As we returned to the antechamber in our new wardrobe Drakeforth asked, "What about the hair and beards?"

Hoptoad smiled. "Only those who are ready to devote their lives to Arthurianism may take that final step to occlude their identity and become one with his holy *Barba*."

"Surely it is the lack of oneness with any barber, holy or otherwise, that puts you in such a sorry state of grooming?" Drakeforth said.

"The word is '*Barba*'. Look it up if you like. Please complete these forMs By signing them you agree to partake in the rites and rituals of the spiritual retreat we offer here. You may leave at any time, but any donation is non-refundable. All we ask is that you respect our beliefs and ponder the teachings we provide."

"That should be fine," I said quickly before Drakeforth could make it worse. "How long does the retreat take?" I added, filling out a form with the pencil provided.

"It does not matter, so long as you are advancing," brother Hoptoad said. Drakeforth gave a snort.

"For the initial experience we suggest you remain as our guests for two or three days. This allows your mind to clear and for the light of our Lord to resonate within you," he continued.

"That sounds lovely," I said, wondering if I would have to stab Drakeforth with the pencil to get him breathing properly again.

We signed the forms and were asked to make a cash donation. Credit sticks made cash superfluous, but any transaction using a stick could be traced and we were trying to stay off the mesh.

"Surely you have a stick-reader?" I asked, determined to play the role of a city-born technophile.

"We shun modern technology. Devices powered with empathic energy are not permitted here."

"How on earth do you live?" Drakeforth asked, completely ignoring the irony of the cash he had used to pay for our food and room.

"In peace and at one with our true natures," Hoptoad replied. "We can, if necessary, provide you with a manual promissory note and take an imprint of your credit stick."

"How barbaric," Drakeforth quipped as he handed over a thin wad of the bank notes he carried in his pocket. The monk didn't even blink.

"How would you add obscurity to clarity?" Hoptoad asked.

After our donations were accepted we returned to the circular hall. The room was filling rapidly with men and women of all ages. Each one knelt at a point around the spiral, creating a third dimension to the pattern. They faced inwards, all faces attuned towards a central point. Hoptoad indicated we should take a place within the gathering. We knelt with the others and waited to see what would happen next.

Hoptoad went to the end of the spiral and began to walk around it. Passing in front of each Arthurian he circumnavigated the room a dozen times, coming closer to the centre with each pass. Finally he reached the central point and turned in a full circle.

"I am with us," he began. "I am within all of us. I am the clothes we wear. The food we eat. The water we drink. I am all of us. I was, I am, and I will be. So Arthur counselled his disciple Saint Forefoot when she asked him what would become of the Octarch when their perception of him altered. Arthur teaches us that nothing exists except change and that it is only our perception that changes. The things we experience are distanced from us by the physical embodiment of our notions. Once we doubt the surety of our senses we can perceive the multiverse. Arthur spoke the truth. With the passing of that which his disciples perceived, he became the earth, the grass, the flesh, the water, the sky. We who strive for a pure understanding of his truth know we must tear ourselves free of our preconceived ideas. There must be emptiness to be filled…"

Hoptoad went on in this vein for over an hour. My feet went

numb first, and I could feel the paralysis creeping up my legs. I wondered what would happen when it reached my head. I pondered whether it were possible to die from numbness-induced asphyxiation.

The elderly monk did not speak using any overtly obvious persuasion techniques, and yet he held the audience in rapt attention with his every word. They nodded and stroked their beards in agreement with his many points.

From what I had read and seen on television, Arthurianism seemed to be a religion based around the sort of odd ideas that aren't normally taken seriously outside of an advanced theoretical quantum physics laboratory.

Hoptoad preached a mix of pseudo-science and rhetoric, sprinkled with instructions on how important it was to be nice to everyone.

Of course, there have been occasions in history when Arthurianism was not characterised by a bludgeoning sense of niceness and had been all about taking up the sword and going on zealous missionary missions.

Hundreds of years ago, militant Arthurians had rampaged across entire countries, converting terrified natives with what became known as the Kebab Choice. That is when a blood-stained lunatic holds a sword to your throat and asks if you have thought about abandoning your current false dogma for the up-and-coming One True Religion of Arthurianism. It proved to be a remarkably successful crusade and Saint Kebab's campaign ran at a conversion rate of nearly a hundred per cent. It would have been a perfect score, if not for an unfortunate cultural misunderstanding with the Took people of the wild and windswept tundra plateau of Upper Besex. The Took shook their heads when they wanted to indicate yes.

I looked for Drakeforth. To my surprise he was curled over, his hands flat on the floor and his face almost touching the polished timber. "What are you doing?" I mouthed.

Drakeforth inhaled through his nose and turned his head to grin up at me. "Patchouli oil," he whispered.

CHAPTER 7

I had to wait until Hoptoad finished his sermon before I could crawl on hands and numb knees over to Drakeforth.

"Patchouli oil," he said with barely restrained excitement as the faithful rose to their feet and slowly moved out of the hall. "The floor reeks of it."

"Maybe they polish the wood with it?" I frowned at the floor.

"It's patchouli oil, not linseed," he said giving me a scathing look that he had probably prepared earlier.

"You are welcome to eat with us," Hoptoad said softly, gliding up on soft-soled sandals.

"That would be lovely, thank you," I replied for both of us and accepted a hand up off the floor from Hoptoad. My legs tingled painfully and the usual aches and numbness in my extremities seemed amplified.

"Do the Arthurians have any dietary restrictions?" Drakeforth asked. His tone of sudden respect and genuine interest took me by surprise. Hoptoad didn't seem to think it strange, but then he hadn't spent an hour with Drakeforth yet.

"We do not consume processed foods that we have not processed ourselves. We will dine on all that walks, crawls, flies, and grows from the ground, the fish of the sea and the fowl of the air."

"So sea birds are off the menu?" Drakeforth couldn't help himself.

"Not at all, we enjoy *Albatros a l'Orange* every Sunday." Hoptoad winked at me in a grandfatherly way that gave me a sharp pang of reminiscence for my own parents.

"You grow all your own food, vegetables and other consumables?" Drakeforth continued with his subtle interrogation as we left the grand hall on slippered feet and made our way to a clutch of smaller buildings beyond the vegetable patch.

"Yes; fruit, vegetables, livestock and cheeses. The only thing we import is salt and sweetener. Fortunately we have monasteries in suitable climates for growing stevia and others in coastal regions with evaporation ponds for salt gathering. Our local specialty is herbal extracts and oils."

"How simply fascinating," Drakeforth said.

In the dining room, long tables were laid with bright bowls of salads and platters of sliced meat. Bread, cheese and jugs of what turned out to be beer were being passed around. The room was filled with amicable chatter and smiling people. We took our seats and our plates were promptly filled. I inhaled the bouquet of fresh herbs, seasoned vegetables and roast chicken. No doubt the hens I had seen earlier furiously foraging for spilled seeds and insects on the monastery grounds were beginning to wonder why this plump lady hadn't been around for the last few days.

The lunch was delicious and the conversation quite ordinary. It seemed Arthurians liked to discuss mundane things over meals: the weather, chicken recipes, and the annoying way that you couldn't hear yourself chew over the noise of all these people talking in the dining hall.

The afternoon was to be spent in further instruction. We met one of Hoptoad's fellow believers, a middle-aged woman with greying hair and a tanned face wrinkled with smile lines.

"This is sister Buddleia," Hoptoad said.

"The future is the continuity of an expression of life," Buddleia said, smiling warmly at us and squeezing my hand between two that were caked in dirt.

"Hello, I'm Charlotte, and this is my friend Vole," I replied.

"Lovely herb garden you have there," Drakeforth said. "I'm something of a keen herbalist myself, mind if I take a look?"

"Perception is the path to incredible energy," Buddleia said and led Drakeforth away to inspect the oregano, the basil and, I fervently hoped, the patchouli.

"Let's go sit in the shade and have a chat," Hoptoad said. I nodded and followed him, not having anything else to do. We took seats in chairs carved from sawn lengths of trees. Hoptoad swept his long hair around his shoulder like a tattered cotton scarf. A jug of iced tea was brought out of the dining hall and set on a wooden table between us. It all felt very civil and entirely unlikely.

"What is your story, Charlotte?" Hoptoad asked gently.

"I—well, I'm just curious I guess. Always looking for an answer to life's big mysteries. Why are we here, where do we come from, what does it all mean, why exactly do we have earlobes…" I trailed off, realising I was babbling.

Hoptoad pondered his feet for a moment. "You are here because you are searching for something. You came from the city. It means exactly what you think it means, and there are two main theories. One is that some distant ancestral mammalian quadruped used them to keep the dirt out of the ear canal and the other is that they may be something to do with sex. Which personally I find a far more intriguing theory, but one perhaps grounded more in wishful thinking than empirical evidence. However, my question was referring to your personal history. You have an air of sadness about you that is tempered by a grim determination."

I took a deep breath. If half of what Drakeforth had told me was true, grim determination might be what I needed. Besides, I mused, what else do I have to live for?

"I believe, no, *we* believe, that the Godden Energy Corporation is somehow involved in a conspiracy. It has to do with the discovery of empathic energy. I think my parents may have been murdered because of a desk that has been in my family for generations. I suppose none of this means anything to you, being self-sufficient and off the mesh and everything." I winced internally. *Do shut up, Charlotte. You are sounding like a complete idiot!*

Hoptoad nodded. "Thirty years ago I walked away from a

career in widget management to answer the call of Arthur. I was overweight, divorced, miserable, and my career seemed to be going nowhere. There was so much wrong with the world we lived in that I ran away. I arrived here, much as you have, and here I stayed." Hoptoad's gaze went to some distant horizon of memory. "I had so many questions, just like you. As for the answers...well, Arthur had only one."

I felt myself leaning forward to hear the wisdom he would share.

"Nothing matters, everything matters." Hoptoad drank some iced tea and we sat in silence. A thousand thoughts circled a dark centre in my mind like a fleet of tiny paper boats caught in the vortex of a drain.

I felt guilty watching the Arthurians working in the warm sun while I sat here in the shade and drank delicious tea.

Drakeforth's head appeared occasionally between the rows of herbage. Together he and Buddleia were like a pair of meerkats popping up from behind the chives and garlic. They would speak briefly, exchange leaves of various shapes and colours and then vanish again. I'd not seen Drakeforth look this relaxed before. If it wasn't for his raging intolerance of all things spiritual, the life of an Arthurian would have suited him perfectly.

"What do you do here, Hoptoad? Other than giving sermons and overseeing everything."

"I'm not in charge. No Monastery of Arthur has a leader. We are simply a group of like-minded individuals who have come together and share a common understanding. We await the fulfilment of Arthur's Tellings."

"You think Arthur will return?"

"He might. He might have never left. He might be among us right now. You might be Arthur."

"I don't think so." I blushed slightly.

"Arthur was a man who made a great assumption. He then devoted his life to proving that assumption to be correct. The core tenets of our faith are curiosity, peace and the acceptance that we are, have been, and always will be, energy in a transient state. Arthur was the first among us to transcend the physical

70

form and attain a different state of existence. We seek to emulate his path and perceive ourselves in a state of existence without boundary or dimension."

"It sounds very challenging," I said, not quite understanding what he was talking about.

"It's quite simple really. You just have to realise some truths about whichever of the infinite number of universes you wish to inhabit, and then accept that reality isn't all that it is cracked up to be."

"Reality." I grasped the one term I could make sense of in his speech. "Let me tell you about reality. It's random and objective and completely uncaring about anything as complex as a person's life." To my surprise, Hoptoad nodded and stroked his beard.

"Or," he replied, "reality is a construct of your perceptions. If you think, and here I quote the common vernacular, reality barks like a dog in a well, then you need to take steps to change it."

"Oh, right. How silly of me. Instead of my parents dying, I should have just changed reality so they didn't."

Hoptoad nodded again. I felt a sudden flash of anger. How dare he sit there and *blame me* for not changing what happened?

"You cannot be seriously suggesting I could have changed my own past?"

"Many of us have a strong desire to change actuality. What we must accept is that the time to change that which *is* remains in the time when it *still might be*. To put it another way, at this moment, and every other moment, you stand at an infinite crossroads. Stretching out from you are an endless number of probable actions, encounters, events and perceptions. Each one represents a different reality, entirely valid in its own wave function. The only time you can choose which of those probabilities you will actualise is before they have come to pass. Once a probability is actualised and becomes your new reality, the others either cease to exist mathematically, or they go off on their own tangents and are experienced by a different you. It all depends on your interpretation of Arthur's Tellings."

My fury subsided somewhat, "So...you are saying the only

way to change the future is to choose a different course of action in the present?"

"Exactly." Hoptoad beamed at me through his whiskers.

"I give up." I waved my hands in exasperation. "The Arthurian doctrines seem horribly fatalistic. I can certainly take responsibility for my own actions, but the idea that my future was basically my fault seems a bit unfair."

"Not at all," Hoptoad responded. "Arthurianism simply suggests you take more care in your current choices."

"But how do I know that the choice I make is the right one?"

"Exactly," Hoptoad said again, leaving me completely baffled.

Drakeforth came striding out of the garden, his white robe damp and dirt-stained in the knee regions. "Can you believe they have allfoot and coffee plants growing back there?"

I smiled agreeably at him. "Coffee?" I asked.

"A bean that can be dried, roasted and ground. It makes an interesting alternative to tea," Hoptoad explained.

"I think I've heard of it," I said.

"Buddleia tells me you make your own patchouli oil." Drakeforth's eye flickered as if he were trying to drop me a wink and only succeeded in looking as if he had a nervous tic.

"Indeed. Perhaps you would both be interested in seeing our botanical oils plant?"

We nodded and once again followed Hoptoad across the wide farmyard inside the monastery's walls. He unlocked a heavy door set in the outer stone wall. From there we passed into cool shadow and started down a long flight of stone steps.

Drakeforth's hand dropped on my shoulder. I nearly screamed. "Paranoia," he whispered. I nodded. The dark and narrow passageway had the hairs on the back of my neck craning for a better view. Ahead of us a match flared and grew into the softer glow of a lamp. Hoptoad's face loomed out of the darkness.

"Mind the last step. It's a bit odd," he said. Turning his back, Hoptoad unlocked a second door. This one had been strapped in bands of iron like an old barrel. The monk held the lantern up until we joined him on the other side of the door. He closed it in our wake, twisting a key in the lock and hanging it up on a wall hook.

Walking on, Hoptoad said, "We produce a range of herb and plant oils. We use most of them in our rites and rituals." Hoptoad paused and bent down to stare carefully at a set of wooden shelves laden with clay jars and glass bottles of all sizes. He reached in and fossicked among them for a moment. "Some are just the thing for adding a little zing to your bathwater." He straightened up and took us deeper into a series of round chambers, their layout and design mirroring the meeting chamber we had communed in before lunch.

"Here is where we manufacture our oils." We stood under a domed roof of fitted stone blocks. Around us were vats, presses and racks of drying plants. The smell rolled over me, a cloying miasma of every perfume I had ever worn.

"Where is the patchouli?" Drakeforth turned around, scanning the room before marching off into the thick of it all.

"This, I am afraid, is going to hurt you a lot more than it is going to hurt me." Hoptoad raised his arm. The object he had lifted from the shelf outside the room slid out of his loose sleeve. The hand that held it pointed, unmoving and perfectly level, at my chest.

CHAPTER 8

"Is that a gun?" I asked, not having seen a real one before.

"Yes," Hoptoad replied. "Yes, I believe it is."

"Isn't that illegal?" I felt the moral high ground was my best defence at this time.

"Defending ourselves against your kind of tyranny is no less legal than the application of the tyranny itself," Hoptoad said.

"Pudding, they have enough patchouli oil back here to—oh…" Drakeforth stepped back into the circle of lantern light and took stock of the situation.

"Hoptoad," I said, automatically utilising the Pendrock Persuasion Paradigm, "please put the gun down." The priest barely twitched.

"Oh, please. The Arthurians invented the science of Dialectics a thousand years ago. You think I can be swayed by the application of a few bumbling intonements?"

Drakeforth chose this moment to throw a spatula at Hoptoad's head. I had no time to consider where such an implement may have come from as it hit the elderly monk between the eyes. He cried out and the gun jerked upwards, firing with a roar and blinding flash.

"Run!" Drakeforth yelled. So I did. Straight at Hoptoad. I tackled him around the middle and crashed us into a stand of wooden barrels. The gun went skittering sideways across the floor, vanishing under the herb drying racks like an embarrassed crab.

Much like a dog chasing cars, now that I had caught Hoptoad,

I was at a loss on what to do next. I gagged on a mouthful of the old man's hair. His surprisingly tough fist crashed into my head and I saw stars before automatically letting go and curling into a foetal position on the floor.

Through a gap between my elbows I saw Drakeforth leap into the fray, wrapping a handful of Hoptoad's flowing locks around the monk's throat and trying to choke the life out of him.

Hoptoad reached over his head and jabbed Drakeforth in the ear with a thumb. Drakeforth's left leg shot out sideways, nearly putting them both on the floor. The monk jabbed again at a slightly different point. This time Drakeforth's hands flew up above his head. He kept his grip on Hoptoad's hair and they both disappeared under the blanket of the monk's white locks. They grunted and thrashed until eventually Drakeforth crawled out and brushed himself off.

My left cheek throbbed in a way that promised an impressive bruise. A brass band played enthusiastically in my head and the fireworks behind my eyes were a sight to behold.

"Are you completely insane?" Drakeforth demanded of the wheezing old man lying at his feet.

"You shan't…get away…with this…" Hoptoad gasped.

"And you thought you could get away with murdering us?" I crawled to my feet and felt the world spinning on its axis.

"Not murder, if for the common good," Hoptoad said.

"Actual common good is all too rare these days," Drakeforth replied.

"You won't shut us down. You can destroy all that we have created here, but we are protected," Hoptoad declared.

Drakeforth's strength returned with a push up from his conviction. He got to his feet and shook the dirt from his hair.

"We don't give a telephonist's trachea what you silly burghers do out here. We just wanted some banjoed patchouli oil!" Drakeforth exploded.

"Really?" Hoptoad did not look convinced.

"Absolutely," I said and the whole story started to come out in a rush, "We tried everywhere in the city, we think that maybe the Godden Energy Corporation has somehow stopped the oil being available. We came here because the police got involved, and the most frightfully sarcastic woman and this creepy little man with an oxyacetylene torch. You see it all started with my great-grand-grandmother's desk and my toaster."

My speech would have a greater impact if I hadn't started crying about halfway through. Whatever else I was going to say was lost in a cloud of blubbering.

"You're not agents of Godden, then?" Hoptoad's scowl took on a questioning aspect.

"Not vexing likely," Drakeforth said.

Hoptoad made a harrumph sound, "You wouldn't believe the trouble we have had with Godden agents over our herbal oils. But tell me, how exactly did you think we could help you?"

"We need some patchouli oil. Drakeforth believes that there is a conversation of grave importance recorded in my great-grandmother's living oak desk," I said, wiping my eyes and feeling foolish.

"And patchouli oil is the only way to extract that which has been preserved in living oak," Hoptoad said, nodding.

"To answer your rhetorical question, yes, we would believe the trouble you have had with the agents of Godden. We've experienced quite a bit of it ourselves," Drakeforth said.

I almost said, *"Well I haven't."* A few days ago my biggest concern was the inevitable downward spiral of my health and affording car repairs.

"This is for real, isn't it?" I asked instead. "There really is a conspiracy and they really do want to stop anyone getting hold of any patchouli oil."

"Agents of Godden. Without a doubt," Drakeforth replied and Hoptoad nodded in agreement.

"I still think if we hadn't run away from the police, I could have explained everything and all of this would have been cleared up straight away." In a rational world, this course of action would have made perfect sense. Now that Drakeforth was involved, it seemed almost absurd.

"I was following *you,"* Drakeforth said, the indignation apparent in his voice. *"You* ran out of the house when the police

showed and then *you* drove the getaway vehicle."

"Do you ever take responsibility for anything?" I seethed.

"I understand free will. You make your choices, I am simply the observer," he replied with an irritating calm.

"That's quite a personal philosophy, Drakeforth. I would like to point out that my life was relatively straightforward until you started following me." I cast about, looking for the spatula or something more adamant to hit him with.

"We can help you," Hoptoad said. "If you are who you say you are. We have the patchouli oil you need."

"I'm right, aren't I?" Drakeforth said. "The Godden Energy Corporation is involved in some grand conspiracy."

"How would I know?" Hoptoad bristled. "I'm just trying to live a simple life connecting to a higher power. Instead I have men in suits turning up and asking about patchouli oil production and suggesting, in no uncertain terms, that we should stop growing the Arthur-given plants we depend on."

"What do you use it for?" I asked.

"Patchouli oil is used for anointing the faithful during our meetings. We also hold a sacred artefact of Saint Detriment. A shard of living oak that holds an exchange between the saint and our lord Arthur himself."

"You actually have the voice of Arthur recorded in living oak?" I felt a chill. "Why has no one ever heard of this?"

"Sacred artefacts are holy iteMs They are not for public consumption or display."

"This conversation between Saint Detriment and Arthur? What do they actually say?" Drakeforth narrowed his eyes.

"It's not really a conversation. We consider it a verbal exchange."

"But it's his actual words? Arthur's actual words?" I said, still trying to get my head around this. There was no doubt that someone called Arthur had once lived; many contemporary histories mentioned him and even his tax records were revered in Taxonomy circles.

Hoptoad sighed, "We hold the sacred living oak table tennis paddle of Saint Detriment, made in the days when living oak was not the conserved treasure it is today.

"So this saint of yours and Arthur were discussing the true nature of man's morality while playing table tennis?" Drakeforth's eyes had narrowed to slits.

Hoptoad took a deep breath, "The sacred words of our Lord Arthur are thus," he intoned. "Three-six. My serve. You can't expect to return a third-ball tight with a smash. A counter-drive is the better stroke against that kind of short backspin."

"Does any of what you do in the name of religion make any sense to you at all?" Drakeforth said.

"Faith answers all the questions that knowledge poses." Hoptoad said with a definite sniff in his voice. Drakeforth gave a frustrated groan and turned on his heel, storming out of the lantern light and back towards the locked door.

"This should suffice." Hoptoad took a bottle labelled 'Patchouli' from a shelf, pulled the cork and held it up to my nose. It smelled earthy.

"Don't worry, it's the real thing," the priest smiled.

"Thank you. This will be of great help."

"However, I cannot let you leave here with patchouli oil. It would be wise for you to bring the desk to us and let it be anointed."

"Is that really necessary?"

"You are on a quest that Arthur has ordained," Hoptoad said.

"Thank you," I said. "You will take care of the desk? If we bring it to you? I mean, I'll get it back, right?"

"Empathic energy is meant to be natural. Converting it to man's desires has enslaved us all. Perhaps with Arthur's guidance we can return to a more natural world."

"What could be more natural than empathic energy?" I frowned at the monk. "Just this once, a straight answer, please."

"Positive human emotions enhance the effectiveness of the double-e flux. We live in a world of peace because the nations of the world realise that it is more efficient to live in a world without strife and war. You need to ask yourself: what price peace on earth and goodwill to all men?"

"What do you mean?" My time at the monastery had helped

me understand why Drakeforth railed against organised religion.

"What is the source of empathic energy? Where do you think it comes from?" Hoptoad asked.

"Well...Godden discovered the double-e flux present in living oak and invented the first empathic energy inverter. From there it was a simple matter of hooking it up to something mechanical and developing more efficient systems and machines." I gave the obvious answer.

"We have always been told that empathic energy was first discovered as part of Godden's experiments with botanical psychiatry. Seeking to measure the emotional responses of plants, he instead discovers a new form of energy," Hoptoad said and I nodded; that was what I learned in school.

"But Godden never studied botany, or psychiatry. He had no interest in plants. He was an engineer. His only interest in plants was researching how to ferment them into grain alcohol and distil unlicensed sunshine for parties. Whatever your friend hopes to learn from your living oak desk, it may be very dangerous. We can keep its secrets safe here."

"Thanks for the warning. We'll be back with the desk as soon as possible." I walked ahead of the lantern light, Drakeforth paced outside the locked door.

"Thanks for waiting," I said.

"Did you get it?" he replied.

"Hoptoad says we should bring the desk here. So it can be properly anointed and they can hide it."

"What buffoonery. Though I suppose hiding the desk here could be safer than leaving it in your home," he said.

"Only if it is still at home. The GEC could have stolen it already."

"We will return to reconnoitre the premises and determine the fate of your family heirloom," Drakeforth announced grandly, and with that Hoptoad unlocked the door and we returned to the surface.

CHAPTER 9

The afternoon sunlight was bright and warming after our sojourn into the underworld. The breeze cleared my head of the cloying stink from the cocktail of drying herbs and extracted oils.

"I'm going to get dressed. Then we can leave this unregistered asylum," Drakeforth announced and strode towards the sermon hall. His swagger made it clear that he did not want to maintain the façade of religious humility any longer. I took my time trailing after him; after all, I had the car keys.

"Is your friend leaving?" Buddleia asked, emerging from her carefully cultivated rows of cinnamon.

"I'm afraid so. Urgent business back in the city. But thank you so much. The monastery is lovely."

"Put this on that bruise, it will help the swelling go down. You should report him to the police and leave him in the same breath."

"What? Oh, the bruise?" I touched my red and swelling cheek. "No, it wasn't Drakeforth. I—I walked into a shelving unit down there in the dark."

"Uh-huh. I am sorry to see you go; I was looking forward to showing you how we make goosefat marmalade."

I blanched a little until the sister stroked a soft, white-furred leafy plant. "Goosefat," she explained.

"Perhaps next time."

After I dressed in my civilian clothes, I waved to the few people I made eye contact with on my way out the gate. As we passed under the ancient wall, the stones themselves erupted with the roaring echo of banshees supporting their favourite football team. I ducked, thinking the ancient blocks were collapsing, as a helicopter thudded overhead and settled in the air outside. On the other side of the wall I saw Drakeforth standing next to the car and waving frantically. I ran for it, the egg-folder drumming of the helicopter blades beating in a manic rhythm overhead. With the air pushing down around us we piled into my little Flemetti and powered out of there in a cloud of dust. The helicopter rose from its low-altitude squat and lunged after us. I drove faster than I dared on the narrow road as it twisted through the trees down the hillside. I could see the occasional flash of chrome and black through the foliage as Drakeforth kept a running commentary on my failings as a getaway driver.

"Go faster! They'll catch us if you don't! This isn't a scenic tour! Change down a gear! Get your revs up! Would you like me to get out and push!?"

I ignored my passenger. The Flemetti was meant for this kind of suicidal driving. She clung to the road like a baby monkey on her mother's back. The engine purred, oblivious to the panic of the occupants. She loved to be off the leash of city driving. Here she could run free and do what she was built for. I felt a tingling sense of excitement ripple through me too. For the first time ever, things felt important. Really important. The choices I made and the actions I took would define what happened next. I pressed my foot down on the throttle.

We shot out of the trees at the bottom of the mountain road and skidded sideways into the wide black band of the highway. There was no question of not going back to the city directly. The helicopter buzzing overhead could follow us anywhere. Beyond the point where we returned home, and possibly had a cup of tea, my planning became more speculative.

We hurtled down the road, zipping in and out of traffic, the polite throat clearing of car-horns sounding behind us.

"They're still coming!" Drakeforth said, twisting around and trying to see out of the car's low windows.

"They might just be going in the same direction as us," I

replied, cutting in between a truck and a family in a Sleeka station wagon.

"Of course, why didn't I think of that?" Drakeforth replied. After a while his sarcasm lost its impact, mostly because every-;thing he said sounded sarcastic.

We hurtled on down the road, cars blurring around us. I felt excitement building deep in my chest. If I was going to die anyway, then what better way to pass? Also, I thought savagely, removing Vole Drakeforth from the gene pool might earn me some kind of posthumous medal. I glanced over at him. Drakeforth was grinning.

"What's got you so amused?" I said, my eyes cutting back to the road.

"We are having an adventure. An actual life-and-death adventure. It's got everything! A mysterious message, a hidden treasure, an evil villain, a stalwart hero with a beautiful sidekick, car chases, gun-fights and daring escapes."

"You're not that beautiful," I said.

His snort was drowned out by the sudden thud of the helicopter rotors roaring louder as the aircraft dropped down in front of the car, turning under the whirring blades until the craft's nose pointed straight at me. Cars and trucks swerved off the road, brake lights flashing. I slammed on the brakes. The car skidded, her petite backside flicking out sideways. I steered into it and straightened up. The helicopter had come close enough to the road to allow a squad of goons in black overalls to jump down and stop traffic.

"Reverse!" Drakeforth yelled. I looked back at the traffic building up behind us. Their headlights glowing in the late afternoon sunshine like a jungle full of angry lemurs. We were already trapped.

"Go round!" Drakeforth yelled again. I gunned the engine and twisted the wheel. We cut around a four-door Sobato and missed taking out the fender wing of a classic Dakata Vroom by inches. Ahead the road got tangled. Cars had pulled aside, assuming some kind of emergency had brought the helicopter down in their midst. Other cars had tried to follow suit, and now found themselves angle-parked across the lanes. The polite coughs of their horns echoed around us. I drove forward as far as I could, the Flemetti's engine growling at the restraint being imposed on her. After another twenty feet we rolled to a halt.

"Get out," Drakeforth ordered. I just looked at him. "Go on, run for it!" He pushed on my arm. I stood, or rather sat, my ground. Where, exactly, was I going to go?

The men and women in black jumpsuits were bearing down on us, pacifier truncheons held tight against their chests. The ring near the truncheons' electrically charged tips glowed blue, indicating they were ready to deliver a stunning blow. I tried to open my door, but there wasn't room with the cars packed in around us, and the guard on Drakeforth's side was too close. We were trapped while curious drivers climbed out of their cars and asked each other stupid questions.

A moment later the more casual end of a pacifier baton tapped on my window. I wound it down and smiled up at a grim-faced young man.

"Good evening, is there some kind of problem?" I asked.

"Miss Charlotte Pudding?" he said.

"Never heard of her!" Drakeforth barked from the other side of the car.

"Mr Vole Drakeforth?" the agent of Godden said, ducking down to stare into the car's low-slung and classically styled interior.

"Never heard of him," I declared.

The agent straightened up and made a waving gesture at his colleagues. They in turn waved towards the helicopter, which lifted off the ground and moved out of the stalled flow of traffic.

"Please turn off your car engine and remain exactly where you are," the young agent said.

"Under whose authority?" Drakeforth demanded.

"Just turn off your engine please, miss."

I obeyed. We sat in guilty silence watching as the traffic jam cleared and each occupant of every passing car turned to stare at us as they passed. Each of them an eye-witness to whatever was happening to us. Of course, no one challenged the men in black.

I knew that in their position I would do the same. If someone who looked like a highly trained security officer was engaged in securing a suspect, the suspect was clearly guilty of something, most likely something despicable.

Finally we were alone, except for the seven men and women in black, wielding pacifier truncheons.

"Step out of the car." I noticed the agent had stopped saying 'miss'. We both climbed out and Drakeforth was immediately pushed to the back of the Flemetti. They made us stand with our backs to each other and I was quickly and thoroughly searched. From Drakeforth's protests he was getting the same treatment.

"Is this gun yours, sir?" I turned to stare at the back of Drakeforth's head. A female agent held up Hoptoad's gun with the same thumb-and-forefinger minimum contact usually reserved for dead rats.

"Never seen it before in my life," Drakeforth said.

"It was in your coat pocket," the agent reminded him.

"I've never seen this coat before in my life either. It could belong to anyone."

The gun was placed in a plastic bag and sealed away and then we were guided towards the helicopter, which had landed in a cow paddock beside the highway. The herd had retreated to a safe distance from which to assess this new thing. They appeared to have reached a consensus that it would be better to ignore the helicopter and go back to eating grass and not bothering with matters beyond their understanding.

We stepped around the steaming remains of the cows' initial shock and climbed into the helicopter. Six agents took up seated positions around us while one remained behind to steal my car.

I had never flown in a helicopter before and it had never occurred to me that when I did, it would be under such strange circumstances. The sensation of lift-off was reminiscent of a strange dream of falling upwards. The initial confusing moment when even gravity was taken by surprise and my internal organs clung to each other in a desperate panic went on for a lot longer than I felt comfortable with. We eventually stopped ascending and flew level. The sun was setting and we soared through the darkness in a black helicopter, surrounded by men and women wearing black. The colour scheme of my thoughts chose conformity over hope.

CHAPTER 10

I roused from my deep despair at the sensation of the helicopter sinking like a bird returning to the nest. We glided into a glowing halo of light that glistened with the lustre of a celebrity engagement ring in the middle of nowhere. I reached out and found Drakeforth's hand, giving it a reassuring squeeze. I looked over to him and realised that sometime during the flight Drakeforth had moved, and now a gruff-looking agent sat between us. He scowled at me until I let go of his hand.

Drakeforth stared out the window into the night sky, oblivious to my embarrassment, which I thought unfortunate; it would have cheered him right up.

"Where are we?" I asked.

"Nowhere," the gruff agent said.

"Any chance I could use the phone?"

"None whatsoever," the agent said.

"Hang on," I snapped. "We have rights, lawyers, phone calls and, ah…memoranduMs" TV cop shows were never my favourite entertainment fare, but it sounded close enough.

"Yes." The gruff agent smiled and leaned in until I could smell the perkhip tea on his breath. "If you get arrested you have rights," he said, grinning into my face.

A sickening feeling cramped my stomach. The agent leaned back, spreading his feet as I leaned over and threw up on their nice black helicopter floor.

We landed a few moments later. I felt too nauseous to apologise. *Serves them right, kidnapping us like this.* I hoped my bile would stain and perhaps corrode some essential electronic component, until one day, long after the search for our remains had been called off and the missing person's case closed, this sleek machine of obfuscation would suffer some catastrophic systems failure and plunge to earth in a spectacular fireball— hopefully with the gruff agent on board.

We were hustled out of the helicopter and onto a cold concrete pad streaked with lines of thick yellow paint. The agents herded us towards a solid-looking door flanked by two armed guards. One of the door guards took two clip-on visitor passes from a box and fastened them to our clothes. The door opened and we passed inside, the sharp acid smell of my vomit becoming more concentrated in the enclosed space of the elevator beyond.

As we descended I felt my stomach roll again. I could almost hear Doctor Hydrangea tsk-tsking. Soon the elevator whispered to a halt. The doors opened and we were marched out into a warm, carpeted room with swirling patterns on the walls and a nice neutral-toned floor covering.

"Welcome to Nowhere." A perfectly presented blonde receptionist stood up from behind her desk and greeted us with a dazzling smile. I nodded weakly; the saccharine greeting and heavy side-arm in her shoulder holster were giving me mixed messages.

"Two for processing," our escort announced.

"Please fill in these forms," the receptionist beamed and we took the offered clipboards. "You can take a seat and wait over there," she added, indicating a leather sofa flanked by two lush pot-plants.

Drakeforth and I sat down, our escort vanishing back into the elevator.

"For an impenetrable fortress of utmost villainy, they have certainly spared no expense on the interior decorating," Drakeforth observed.

"Could you get me a glass of water, please?" The strain of the day's adventure had left me feeling weak and the burning taste of acid made my throat raw. Drakeforth returned to the receptionist and came back with a glass of water a moment later.

"She asked if you need medical attention," he reported.

"Tell her I do. I need to go home and take some painkillers and get a good night's sleep. We can come back at a more mutually convenient time." I blinked as Drakeforth turned on his heel and went back to deliver my sarcasm personally. I sipped the cool water and waited to see what would happen. Drakeforth duly returned.

"She regrets that we will need to remain here until we are summoned and someone will be with us shortly. I wonder what her mother thinks she does for a job?" he added.

"I bet she was popular in school," I replied, feeling strangely numb. Part of me wanted to scream and yet I felt crushed by a sense of hopelessness.

"Yes." Drakeforth slumped into the comfy couch beside me and we glared at the receptionist, who did receptiony things with a tablet computer at her desk and otherwise ignored us.

"I'll bet she got good grades," Drakeforth said.

"And she was on the volleyball team," I offered, remembering those impossibly long legs.

"Captain of the volleyball team. Two years running," Drakeforth folded his arms and smiled gleefully.

"Which still left her with time to win all those swimming medals and get good grades," I said. She had that kind of look about her. The kind of girl who went through her entire teens without ever once having a pimple or having to request permission to leave class to see the school nurse about a tampon.

"Oh, and the family holidays they had." Drakeforth gestured in the air with his pen.

"Winter and summer. Extreme sledding on Mount Cenacle for Hibernal, and then water boarding in the Petrichor Islands during the summer solstice."

"She's the younger of two children."

"Fraternal twins," I corrected with a small laugh. In an entirely irrational way, focusing on something as implausible as the perfect receptionist took my mind off the coma-inducing terror of our situation.

"Her brother was born seven minutes before her and never

lets her forget it," Drakeforth said.

"Of course not. They competed all throughout their childhood," I replied.

"Yet after all this time they still get together with family every holidays, just like old times. New things to debate, new ideas to test and vex each other with. Mother and Father are still so proud." Drakeforth wrote 'Other' in the section for gender.

"Except their parents aren't getting any younger and want grandchildren, but careers come first. It's hard for their perfect children to slow down long enough to find someone to truly fall in love with. The having-kids kind of falling in love," I said, growing more enthralled by this game.

"They keep telling themselves they have time. But they have graduated college now, and are both working in stable corporate jobs with management progression opportunities." Drakeforth signed the box that confirmed the information he had provided on the form was true and correct.

"She is so focused on reaching the top of the corporate ladder she has forgotten to make time to live." A pang of sadness took the fun out of the game. I sank into the deep leather cushions and we stopped making up stories at the receptionist.

"What is going to happen to us?" I murmured.

"Interrogation, I shouldn't wonder," Drakeforth replied.

"They're going to ask us questions?" I asked uneasily.

"Lots of questions."

"But..." and now my fear threatened to choke me, "I don't know anything."

"Don't be so self-depreciating," Drakeforth replied. "You know lots of things. You are an intelligent and highly educated woman."

"Thanks, but you know what I mean."

Drakeforth sighed and balanced the tip of the pen on his finger.

"We know that things are not as they seem. Your desk holds a secret that certain people will kill to protect."

"Kill?" I squeaked. "No one said anything about killing anyone."

"They will, if we don't stop them first."

That sense of panic came charging back and started tossing my mental furniture around.

"I admit, I had less than savoury thoughts on the way in, but, seriously? You are suggesting we kill someone?"

Drakeforth raised an eyebrow, "You have a very limited understanding of death."

"I have had enough experience with it, thank you very much. I'm not going to kill anyone, regardless of the justification."

"What about a thing? Not a person, but a thing?" Drakeforth murmured.

"You don't kill things, you…disconnect them," I replied.

"Well, then, we may have to disconnect someone before this is done," Drakeforth said.

The receptionist answered her phone and then hung up. Standing, she walked towards us on her long, volleyball captain's legs.

"If you will please come with me," she said, plastic smile firmly in place. We clambered out of the couch and handed her our clipboards. Mine had doodles on it of helicopters crashing in monochrome fireballs while agent-sized body parts disintegrated in the spinning rotors. The receptionist took the forms without comment and guided us to a door. It hushed open as she swiped her access card across the sensor and she indicated we should enter the hallway beyond. We stepped forward.

"Tobin," she said to our backs, "was born four minutes before me. And you are right, he never lets me forget it." Her voice cracked slightly and she turned away. The door hissed closed.

"Damn," said Drakeforth. "She seemed so much like a seven minutes younger twin." I shrugged and we walked onto the highly polished black stone tiles that lined the corridor, the light strips overhead glowing as we approached and dimming again in our wake. Further along the walls an avenue of statues was arranged in a bizarre parody of evolution. The first figures were simple tin men, life-sized toys of cylinders and cold headlamp eyes. Beyond these crude prototypes the figures became more refined, taking on human characteristics until they stood proud and victorious, frozen in poses of athleticism and expressions of noble contemplation.

"Who do you think they are?" I asked Drakeforth.

"Perfect ideals?" he suggested. "The faces are all similar. It's a family freak show, or one person's ego."

"It's creepy," I watched the statues as we passed, waiting for them to turn their heads and stare at us. I breathed easier once we reached the end of the strange avenue and approached another closed door. 'Joy Opens Doors', a sign on this one said.

"I wonder if joy is a brand of plastic explosive." Drakeforth said dryly. I put my hand out and touched the portal's surface. It felt warm and quivered under my fingertips.

"I think it's more an instruction. We would like to come in, please," I said with sugar syrup in my voice. The door opened, emitting a purr-like whisper.

"Thank you," I said as we passed through.

The room beyond wanted for nothing, except perhaps more space, a decent view of the countryside and more furniture. Like the other spaces we had passed through since arriving by helicopter, this room had the snug, blank decor of a freight elevator.

Dilby Pretense looked up from the office's single desk and then went back to the documents he was reading.

"Sorry to keep you waiting," he said without looking up again. "Terribly busy, you understand."

"Perhaps we could come back at a more convenient time?" I said, allowing an unaccustomed sauce of sarcasm to marinate my words.

"Absolutely," Drakeforth nodded. "I'm busy for the next hundred years or so, but after that, drop me a mail."

"Ahh-haa," Pretense snickered through his nose and closed the folder in front of him. "Now, where were we?" he asked, standing up and coming to meet us in the middle of the room.

"We were just leaving?" I suggested.

"Introductions would be best, I think. Miss Pudding and I have met, but I don't believe we have had the pleasure, mister...?"

Drakeforth looked at Pretense blankly then roused himself,

"Oh. When you said pleasure, I assumed you were speaking of something else entirely."

"Vole Drakeforth, this is Dilby Pretense. He conducted my recent empathy testing."

"The pleasure is entirely yours, I assure you," Drakeforth said and ignored Pretense's offered hand.

"Miss Pudding, I must say it is delightful to see you again. Your empathic resonators are most extraordinary." Dilby beamed at me.

"Thanks…" I replied, unsure what that meant or what it had to do with our meeting being delightful.

"Exactly how extraordinary?" Drakeforth asked, his eyes narrowing.

"Well on the Marberg Scale, she's a nine point seven eight."

"Nonsense. Your testing equipment is faulty," Drakeforth retorted.

"That's what we thought, but every time we ran the analysis, it came out the same."

"How can I be so high?" I asked.

"We have no idea, but it is fascinating. You are certainly not living up to your empathic potential in your current role." Pretense beamed at me again.

"The highest recorded ER was seven point six. And even that was not widely accepted," Drakeforth said.

"The GEC has the best measuring systems in the world Mr Drakeforth. As we like to say, *we know how you feel*."

"Oh, you have no idea," I muttered.

"So that is why we are here?" Drakeforth asked. "Because you wanted to tell Pudding about her high empathy resonance?"

"Oh no," Pretense snickered again, "we want to conduct further tests. There is also the matter of a certain artefact that she has in her possession."

"The desk," I said, irritating myself further by stating the blindingly obvious.

"Yes," Pretense beamed. "We would like to remove it from your possession."

Hope flared in me as I realised that could only mean that the

Godden Energy Corporation hadn't managed to take it from the vault. "And if I say no?" I asked warily.

"That would be unfortunate," Pretense frowned.

"What if I said no?" Drakeforth asked, his tone more aggressive.

"Well, I'm not sure—" Pretense started. Drakeforth stepped into his personal space like he wanted to dance.

"No," Drakeforth said, staring Pretense in the eye.

"I—I understand that there is some emotional attachment, but this is a unique case. It requires closer study."

"No," Drakeforth repeated firmly.

"But—OW!" Pretense yelped as Drakeforth tapped him on the nose with one finger.

"No," Drakeforth said again.

"The desk has been in my family for generations. I have no interest in or desire to give it up," I interjected. Pretense gave another of his irritating nasal chuckles.

"The desk is a national treasure, therefore neither your interest nor your desire carries any real weight."

"Excuse me?" I said, my voice shrill with incredulous indignation.

"The desk must be handed over to us. There is simply no choice in this matter."

"There is always a choice," Drakeforth announced.

"I refuse to give up the desk," I said, as if it would somehow make my decision clear.

"Is there some aspect of 'national treasure' that I need to explain to you?" Pretense asked.

Drakeforth made a choking sound deep in his throat. "I'm sure this witty repartee could go on all day. But I have a question."

Pretense and I both looked at him, "Why haven't you got the desk already?" he asked.

The balding man blinked behind his glasses, "We can't simply steal it," Pretense said, aghast.

"Of course you can! You people have been stealing things for over a hundred years!" Drakeforth snapped.

"This is a very delicate matter," Pretense said. "I accept it may take you some time to understand your place within the greater plan. I would ask that you take some time to reflect on our request before agreeing to hand the desk over."

"We are leaving. Now," Drakeforth growled.

"Of course. Accommodations have been arranged. I'll summon someone to show you the way." Pretense returned to his desk and summoned a security escort. The door shushed open and two burly guard types turned sideways to enter the room together.

"Accommodations?" I frowned. "We're not staying here. I'm going home. I have to go to work tomorrow."

"Please show our guests the way to their rooms," Pretense said. The two guards nodded and indicated the door. Drakeforth and I exchanged glances before marching out of the office.

"Until next time!" Pretense called after us and waved cheerfully.

The corridor with the timeline of statues seemed longer on the way back. Drakeforth frowned at the various figures, each one perfect and reaching for some lofty, invisible goal.

"These are quite remarkable," Drakeforth said, turning slowly to take them all in.

"The later ones look almost human," I agreed. Drakeforth went in for a closer look.

"Oh, it appears the heads on these are loose."

"Please step away from the statue, sir." One of the guards reached for his pacifier baton.

"Perhaps the poses are designed to be changed, so they don't get bored?" I suggested.

"I think you might be right. The arms and legs are articulated too."

"Sir, I must insist you step down from the pedestal!" The guards stepped forward, batons whining as they powered up.

"Oops," said Drakeforth and shoved hard on the back of the figure he was examining. With a metallic shriek the statue tilted and crashed down, striking one of the guards across the temple with its outstretched metal hand and knocking him out cold. The other guard leapt back. Drakeforth sprang at him, grabbing the first guard's pacifier and tapping the second fellow neatly on the nose. A flash, a squeal, and the guard dropped, convulsing on the floor like a trout doing the limbo.

Drakeforth crouched and took the stunned guard's access card and pacifier. Together we hurried down the corridor.

"What about Miss Perfect?" I said.

"Do you think she has forgiven us for deconstructing her entire life?" Drakeforth asked.

"Would you?"

Drakeforth skidded to a halt on the polished floor. "Good point. There must be another way out of here."

We hurried back the way we came. The guard's access card worked on the first door we came to—a janitor's closet. We moved on to the next one, which was a stairwell going up and down.

"Which way?" I asked, looking back to see if we were being pursued.

"Can you fly a helicopter?" Drakeforth said.

"Of course not."

"Then we go down." Drakeforth let the door seal behind us and we made our way down the concrete stairs. Five floors later we reached the bottom of the shaft. I had no idea if we were above ground or below it. The only indicator of level was the different colours on the doors at the landing of each stairwell.

He opened the door and peered out, "We are in luck, this appears to be a garage. And that means an exit to the nearest roadway."

"Can you see any guards? Security cameras? Attack mongooses?" I said from my frustrated position behind Drakeforth.

"Not that I can see. Unless you have a cobra in your pocket, which should bring them out." Drakeforth cleared the doorway and I let it swing closed behind us.

The concrete ceiling glowed with the same recessed lights as the hallways. We walked down the lane between vehicles like a couple out shopping for a new car.

"Here!" I said. Parked between two hulking great Huge-Machine trucks, my Flemetti crouched like a little dog at a water dish flanked by Rottweilers.

"Fantastic," Drakeforth said. "You have the keys, right?"

I patted myself down like I was spontaneously combusting.

"No…" I wailed. "I left them in the car." We cupped hands on the windows and looked inside. No keys.

"What do you know about hot-wiring cars?" Drakeforth asked.

"As much as I know about the mating habits of the Siberian Koala."

He gave me a pained look, "Sarcasm in the hands of an amateur is an ugly thing."

I tried the driver's side door. It was locked. I snarled in frustration and turned around so I could kick something else. The HuMa truck's panels were armoured, and pain shot up to my knee. "Ow…" I moaned. The Flemetti's locks popped open.

"How…?" I started to ask through teeth gritted against the pain.

"Give me a hand," Drakeforth said. "We'll roll her out and see if we can push-start it." He leaned over and opened the driver's side. I walked backwards twisting the steering wheel, the car rolling smoothly out into the concrete lane.

"Get in, when I tell you, drop the clutch and give it some throttle."

I slid in behind the wheel and waited for Drakeforth's shout. The car rolled forward in silence, "Now!" Drakeforth called. I let the clutch out and pressed down on the throttle pedal. The car jerked and shuddered before grinding to a halt. Drakeforth jerked the passenger door open. "What did you do?"

"Exactly what you told me to do!" I snapped back.

"Pop the hood." he went around to the front of the car. I pulled the lever and the view ahead vanished behind polished red paint. I got out and joined Drakeforth looking in the engine bay. The empathic engine looked as unfathomable to me now as it did when Liz the autotherapist examined it.

"Do you know anything about cars?" I asked.

"Do I know anything about cars?" Drakeforth gave a snort and reached in and wiggled a rubber hose. "Do I know anything about cars," he repeated, poking at something else. "Not a bongo thing," he concluded.

"Hello, car," I said, placing my hands on the smooth cover of what might have been the main e-flux resonator. "I really need you to start. Could you do that for me?" The car sat silent.

"I didn't know Flemetti made a voice-activated model," Drakeforth said.

I ignored him and leaned in closer to the cold engine, "Please," I whispered. "It's very important." The engine trembled and purred into life. I straightened up, knocking my head on the inside of the hood in my surprise. "Thank you," I said, rubbing the back of my skull.

We closed the hood and piled into the car. I gunned the throttle, feeling the engine respond. "Good girl," I said to her.

Drakeforth sighed, "Yes, very clever, now can we get the hay bale out of here?" A shout came from behind us. Guards were spilling into the parking level, batons and other weapons at the ready. Shots rang out and chips of concrete spanged from the pillars.

"Hang on," I said with a grin. Dropping the car into gear we laid a streak of black rubber on the concrete and howled down the lane, cars and trucks flashing past. At the end I spun the wheel and, tyres screaming, we skidded around the corner and roared down the second straight.

"Exit," said Drakeforth, clipping his seatbelt on.

"Got it." We slid into a right-hand turn and blasted up the long ramp, tripping a sensor that sent the door at the top rattling down as we flew towards it. I grinned as Drakeforth sunk down in his seat.

"We're not going to make it! We're not going to make it!" he yelled from his vantage point.

"Come on, girl," I whispered. We shot through the gap, the roof of the low slung car missing the swooping door by an inch.

The yard outside was filled with mysterious crates of an industrial type. The darkness made it hard to see the specifics of whatever the Godden Corporation was using this place for.

"Go that way," Drakeforth said, pointing to a narrow roadway between two shipping containers. The Flemetti zipped along, her headlights blazing in the night.

More shots were fired at us, lights flashed and the steady beams of searchlights speared the darkness. Any moment one of them would nail us to the tarmac like an insect pinned to a card.

Headlights flashed and heavy engines roared as HuMa trucks zipped past on the other side of the stacked containers. We drove around the giant steel blocks in a high-speed game of hide and seek.

"Stop! Back!" Drakeforth barked. The car skidded to a halt. I slammed the gear stick into reverse and shot backwards. A moment later a truck thundered through where we had been scant seconds before.

"Go! Go!" Drakeforth yelled. I moved the gear stick into first and we tore out into the maze of containers again. A man ran out of the darkness and bounced over the front of the car. I screamed as he passed through the flash of our headlights and rolled off the hood of the car without a sound. I stamped on the brakes, looking horrified in the rear-vision mirror. The man we had hit sprang to his feet and start running after us.

"Do not stop!" Drakeforth shouted, twisting in his seat and staring at the pursuing figure. "He certainly isn't!"

The face of the man running after us was expressionless and entirely focused on the chase. I didn't know what Pretense would do with us when we were caught. My imagination could not conjure anything as terrible as that blank face promised. We cut across another intersection and the night vanished in a flare of lights as a HuMa bore down on us. I checked the mirror again in time to see the heavy truck shoot through the crossing, smashing into the running man and knocking him from view.

"Go left," Drakeforth said. I drove as fast as I dared down the narrow gaps between the shipping containers. We only slowed down as we approached a closed gate nestled in a high fence next to a guard booth.

"I hope you have a plan," Drakeforth said.

"I plan on going home," I replied, still in the grip of an adrenaline rush. The car slid to a halt in a spray of gravel before the fence. A man wearing a black flight suit and a bored expression stepped out of the guard house and approached us. The beam of an electric torch flicked over the Flemetti's panels.

"Nice wheels," he said leaning down to the driver's window.

"Thanks," I replied.

"ID?"

"Here," I passed over the door access card we had taken from the unconscious guard. He flashed the torch over it and then directed the light back in my face.

"When did you shave the beard, Milton Burrito?"

I laughed and blinked at him, "I'm sorry. Obviously I'm not Milton, but I've been asked to do a pizza run."

The guard with the torch turned the beam on Drakeforth. "They sure make them look

life-like," he said.

"Amazing, isn't it," I agreed, completely baffled.

"Hey, can you make him say something?" the guard grinned.

"Uhh…Sure. Say hello to the nice man," I ordered Drakeforth.

Drakeforth slowly turned his head and regarded us with soulless eyes. "Thankfully the guard appears to be developmentally challenged," he intoned.

"Oh yeah, there's no way you could mistake that for a real person," the guard laughed and slapped his thigh. "No fungi on my pizza, I'm allergic." He stepped away from the car and pushed a button in his phone-booth-sized box. The gate slid open with an agonising slowness.

"Back soon!" I floored the throttle and we tore out onto a single-lane road that wound through the trees and joined the highway after five miles.

CHAPTER 11

We rolled up the street with the headlights off and stopped the car opposite my front gate. Peering over the driver's door sill we watched my house for a full minute. It didn't move.

"Seems quiet," I ventured, becoming aware of Drakeforth's body pressing against my arm.

"I think that is just the neighbourhood. I'll bet the most exciting thing to happen in these parts is the weekly garbage collection."

I opened my mouth to scoff and then remembered that old Mrs Alpine in number 12 liked to sit in her front room, doing her knitting and watching the garbage trucks emptying the bins every Wednesday.

"Some people like the quiet," I said instead.

"Some people live their entire lives without ever questioning anything. We, my dear Pudding, are not those kinds of people."

"Certainly not," I agreed.

"So, do you want to go first?"

"Certainly not," I said again.

Drakeforth sighed and slipped out of the car. I wondered if I should wait, engine running, ready to tear off through the late evening traffic at a moment's notice if the police, or Godden's agents, or the acerbic Anna Coluthon should prove to be lurking in the shadows of my airing cupboard.

Drakeforth knocked on my window. "Are you coming or what?"

We crept into the house through a brand new front door. The idea of someone restoring the illusion of normalcy after the police had kicked it in chilled me to the core.

Inside I sniffed the air; the usual comforting and familiar scents of home underlaid with the remnant odours of acetylene gas, pipe smoke and vigorous cleaning.

"Can you open the vault?" Drakeforth whispered.

"Of course I can. Shouldn't we check that no one is here first?"

"If you like. You unlock, I'll search."

I turned on the hall light and peered into the retinal scanning lock of the broom cupboard. It beeped and I spun the big wheel open. Several perfectly balanced tonnes of hardened steel and titanium swung out on silent hinges.

My home office was an oasis of calm silence, the desk waiting for me inside as it always had. I wanted to crawl into it and pull the roller top down over me. Drakeforth hadn't returned. I went looking for him.

The kitchen was as we had left it, a cold pot of tea and two empty cups, the chocolate biscuits on the plate going softly stale.

"Drakeforth?" I asked quietly. No response.

I opened the fridge, a reflex distraction brought on by the confusing anxiety of recent events. The fridge didn't say anything. I stared into its cool white interior. "Oh no! Drakeforth!" I shouted.

Slamming the fridge shut, I ran out of the kitchen and up the hall stairs. I reached the top landing and the doors to my bedroom, the bathroom, and the two other bedrooms that waited for the serendipitous arrival of guests since I moved in. Drakeforth lay face-down on the carpet, half out of the bathroom doorway.

"Drakeforth!" I dropped to my knees and turned him over; he groaned, his eyelids fluttering.

"Logout," he mumbled.

A dark shape detached itself from the shadows and I heard a metallic click.

"Stand up please, Miss Pudding," said a confident male voice, the kind of voice that expected to be obeyed without question. I stayed where I was.

"We need to call an ambulance. Drakeforth is hurt."

"Not hurt, simply rendered useless," the voice said. "It wasn't that big a job to be honest. Vole Drakeforth has never served much of a purpose."

"He's saved my life once already," I said, coming to Drakeforth's defence.

"Probably by accident. He's quite comfortable, I assure you. We can lay him out in the guest bedroom if you prefer. But honestly, I'd rather maintain my position of tactical superiority."

"Take his legs," I said, lifting Drakeforth enough to drag him clear of the bathroom. The shadow sighed and stepped over Drakeforth's ankles. I could see now that the man wore a dark trench coat with the collar turned up and a wide-brimmed hat of black felt. Slipping a silver-coloured wand with a needle protruding from the tip into his coat pocket, he seized Drakeforth's legs and together we got him off the floor and into the guest bedroom. With some manoeuvring we levered him onto the bed.

"No, thank you," the man said, adjusting the snap brim of his hat so it continued to hide his face.

"I was just going to ask if you would like a cup of tea."

"I know, and I was pre-empting that by saying no, thank you. I've drunk plenty of tea today awaiting your return."

"You bought fresh milk. I saw it in the fridge."

"Yes, your refrigerator has issues," he declared.

"You should have seen my old toaster."

"I knew you were something special after you felt the distress of the old Python building."

"Who are you?" I asked. His absurd sense of drama beginning to really grate.

"Diphthong, the engineer from the Python building."

"You were with Mr Mulligrubs. Wait, you work for Empathy Tech Services? You're a Godden employee."

"Yes, but my true purpose there is to infiltrate the organisation. There are others who share Vole Drakeforth's concerns about empathy technology. We are trying to find the truth, just as you are. We want to educate people as to what is really going on."

"Why on earth did you knock Drakeforth out?"

"I simply injected him with a sedative."

"Because?"

"I've never had a chance to use the needle gun before. I wanted to try it out."

I stared at the young engineer, completely speechless.

"It worked really well," he said. "I invented it. It needed testing, and Drakeforth needed calming down."

"He saved my life today." I felt this was worth repeating.

"Brother Hoptoad contacted us and said you were being chased by Godden agents in a helicopter."

"How did he know it was a Godden Energy Corporation helicopter?" I said.

"Who else would give a tartan trombone where you go and what you do with your time?"

"You, apparently," I snapped.

"*We*. I am not alone. We are an underground organisation dedicated to bringing the truth to light."

"Where are the rest of you?" I looked around the small bedroom. Other than us, and the lightly snoring Drakeforth, the room stood empty.

"They are organising things. Underground," he said.

"Why are you here, then?" I found myself whispering so as not to disturb Drakeforth.

"Because you are in danger."

"No kidding!" I threw my hands up and went downstairs, Diphthong on my heels.

"I'm not kidding," he insisted.

"What do you know about danger? Particularly relating to me?" I stood in the kitchen and folded my arMs

"We believe that agents of Godden may try to steal the living oak desk that has been in your family for several generations. Our research indicates that it may contain some information that the Godden Corporation does not want made public."

"How long have you been working on this?" I asked.

"Oh, months and months. We have had our top people on it," Diphthong said.

"Great procrastinating pandas," I muttered. I pressed my palms against my eyeballs and took several deep breaths. Pointing out that the Godden Energy Corporation could have stolen the desk at any time during the last two days seemed like a waste of energy.

"I realise this must come as quite a shock to you, Miss Pudding," Diphthong said, his face racked with concern.

"The hardest bit is coming to terms with how completely incompetent you are. Instead of dropping me a note, or warning me weeks ago, you turn up tonight. After—not before, mind you, but *well after* my life has been through the kind of turmoil usually reserved for a potato in a chip factory!"

"We had to be cautious. We may be under surveillance," Diphthong said defensively.

"Under surveillance? I was a prisoner of the Godden Energy Corporation until a few hours ago. Just what have you been investigating? What conspiracy are you and your so-called organisation focused on?"

"We suspect that empathic energy is more than positive emotions and is in fact some secret source of power for the Godden Energy Corporation. We think they are using people," Diphthong said.

"Well of course they are using people! GEC are the biggest employer in the country!"

"Not as employees, but as an energy source. They take the souls of the living and turn them into raw empathic energy."

I blinked. Of all the whacked-out and ridiculous notions that ever hit me in the backside like a squirt of icy bidet water. "You think that empathic energy is actually people? Real people. Not just happy thoughts and positive connections with empowered technology?"

"We are sure of it," Diphthong said nodding. "Independent laboratories have been unable to replicate the synthesis of the double-e flux. GEC refuses to share any details, citing commercial sensitivity."

"Where are the missing person reports? Where are the bodies?" I demanded.

"We're not sure. But they are getting their empathic energy from somewhere. This is a global corporate citizen with over one hundred years of experience in encouraging people to not ask questions. What do you care where your energy comes from provided your hairdryer works or your car runs cheaply?"

He was right. No one cares. We only notice when our cars stop running, or the toaster eats the toast.

"I can assure you I am well aware of the danger I am in. I'm not sure you can help, and frankly right now I am too tired to care. I'm thinking of following Drakeforth's example and going to sleep. Maybe when I wake up the world will be different." I showed Diphthong to the door. He assured me that his group would keep my house under surveillance as regularly as possible and protect me from harm, depending on their availability. He was explaining how they were putting together a roster system when I thanked him and closed the door in his face.

I closed the vault and spun the lock shut before heading upstairs. Drakeforth hadn't moved, so I went to my room and passed out on my bed. My last conscious thought was, *Tomorrow can't be any worse.*

CHAPTER 12

Dawn brought the usual muscle weakness, lethargy and voicemail from Doctor Hydrangea requesting I make a follow-up appointment to discuss the latest test results. Ignoring all three was my way of refusing to accept the obvious, if not the inevitable.

I showered and dressed in fresh clothes. I encountered Drakeforth on my way downstairs. He stumbled out of the guest room, looked at me with wild and confused eyes and stumbled into the bathroom, slamming the door in his wake. I went downstairs and prepared tea and toast. When he emerged, washed and combed, we ate breakfast in silence.

"Why haven't the police come back?" Drakeforth said eventually.

"Why haven't the agents of Godden followed us and dragged us back to whereever that place was? And why is the desk still here? They could have stolen it at any time while we were gone," I replied.

"Two reasons come to mind. Well, one for the police—clearly they have been told to stay out of it. Pretense seemed adamant that they would not steal the desk; you had to hand it over. I think perhaps the Godden Corporation is waiting to see what we do next. If they were prepared to steal the desk then we would no longer be relevant."

"They haven't taken the desk. I don't know why. I would think that was what they were going to do the day they kicked my front door in."

"Then why did they replace the door afterwards? Are we a threat?"

I put down my half-eaten toast, the bread sticking in my throat. "How can we be a threat?"

"There is something about the desk that they don't want anyone to know, but at the same time they don't dare destroy it," Drakeforth mused.

"We can return to the Monastery of Saint Detriment and get Brother Hoptoad to hide the desk. That should be the end of it," I said. Despair, and the idea of risking life and limb for something as absurd as an antique desk, had drained the last of my energy.

"Are you okay? You look paler than usual." Drakeforth sounded genuinely concerned for the first time.

I mustered a smile and said, "I'm fine, just didn't sleep very well."

"If we break the desk up, reducing its mass would reduce the co-efficient of the double-e flux and therefore—"

"Render the desk completely useless. Yes I understand how Marbeld's Law of Reducing Cognisance works."

"As long as Pretense doesn't have the desk, we don't need to steal it back," Drakeforth mused, ignoring my interruption for once.

"But why doesn't Pretense have the desk?" I sighed in frustration. "Why did they say I need to hand it over, and then say I had no choice? You can't ask someone to do something and then tell them they have no choice. It kind of negates the entire purpose for asking them to do something in the first place."

"Unless..." Drakeforth's eyes narrowed, "They had no choice."

"Oh good grief," I muttered, and poured myself a fresh cup of tea.

"Your desk is living oak, the original, natural empathic material. From the mighty oak came many timber house frames, wooden corkscrews, souvenir desk lamp bases—and when people realised what it was worth, there was talk of turning chips of the stuff into currency."

"I don't think my family ever kept the desk a secret," I replied.

"We didn't encourage people to come and paw over it either, mind you." I sipped my tea.

"And for as long as your family has had the desk in their possession, no one has tried to buy, borrow or bugle off with it?"

"As far as I know." I drank more tea, sure that Drakeforth would reach his point eventually.

"Living oak. It gives off a natural double-e flux field. It affects and is affected by people around it."

"Apparently." I wondered if having a chocolate biscuit so soon after breakfast would be frowned upon.

"Well, you understand why they need you to hand over the desk then." It took me a moment to realise that Drakeforth was making a statement, not asking a question.

"Uhm…yes?" I tried. Given what I had been through the last few days, I felt I had earned a chocolate biscuit. Maybe even two of them…

"Pudding, pay attention. You have an empathic quotient off the charts. You spent a considerable amount of time forming a bond with a natural source of empathic energy. That goes two ways. The desk has a bond with you. Without your presence, the desk simply won't function."

"The desk's form is its function, Drakeforth. You pull up a chair and use it as a platform for putting papers on. Besides, it muttered a few recorded words for you."

"Ah!" Drakeforth raised a finger in victory, "But you were present and curious to hear what the desk had to say."

"If what you are saying is true, can we expect the agents of Godden to kick in my door again any moment and take me and the desk into custody?" The tea in my tummy curdled a little at the thought.

"Hoptoad's solution is the best one." Drakeforth stood up and started pacing my kitchen. "We hide the desk at the Monastery of Saint Detriment. We slip it out of the house and spirit it away, so you can be with it in peace and quiet and patchouli oil. We would need some people to help shift the desk. It's quite heavy," Drakeforth concluded.

"We could hire a truck. What we really need is someone who

specialises in the removal of antiques…" I trailed off, a horrible thought coming to mind. My appetite gone, I stood up and started loading the dishwasher, which burbled happily at the attention.

"They wouldn't raise the suspicions of Godden agents," Drakeforth said.

"What if they are Godden agents? Even if they aren't, and we hire them to steal the desk, they will simply take it somewhere to be locked away forever. Or break it up and burn it!" Neither option bore thinking about.

"I have a plan," Drakeforth grinned.

"Did you ever think that life would be so much easier if you had a hamster called Clarence instead?" I asked hopefully.

"Theoretically, if hamsters were not kept in cages and ultimately neglected by forgetful children, they would breed at such a prodigious rate as to take over the world. Entire ecosystems would be threatened by plagues of the small rodents."

"We could always farm them for food, and then use their skins to make very small shoes and handbags."

Drakeforth regarded me steadily, "Pudding, there are times when I don't think you take me at all seriously."

I straightened up from the dishwasher. "Drakeforth. I swear I have never taken anything more seriously in my life than your concern for the environment."

"I think you should call the couple with the interest in antiques," Drakeforth said.

I recognised Benedict's voice when he answered on the second ring. "EGS Benedict and Associates."

"Mister Benedict? It's Charlotte Pudding. I'm calling you about the unresolved agony of a certain possession." I tried not to look at Drakeforth, who was silently applauding in the background.

"Miss Pudding, I am so pleased you called." Benedict sounded intrigued.

"Could you come with your assistant and remove it from the premises? I need it gone. Today, if possible." I could hear the muted snapping of fingers and rustling of papers on the other end of the line.

"Ah, let me see. Would right now suit you?" Benedict asked.

"I guess. I…I'm not sure how much longer I can hold on…" I stifled a sob and waved frantically at Drakeforth, who was miming playing a violin.

"We understand, Miss Pudding. Your emotional stability is our only concern. We will see you shortly."

I hung up and Drakeforth's laughter filled the kitchen. "You should be an actor," he declared.

"This had better work," I said.

"Of course it will work. What can one very small man and one unpleasant woman do against the might of two crusaders for truth such as us?"

I didn't have time to start listing all my concerns. Instead we moved on to what Drakeforth called phase two of the operation.

Drakeforth vanished into the office. It was a small and cluttered space, and I couldn't think where he might hide. I paced up and down, rehearsing a dozen speeches, feeling a range of emotions and convincing myself that this was all going to end badly.

When the doorbell rang I managed not to scream. I did manage to answer it, and found myself belt to nose with the well-practiced and deeply concerned expression of EGS Benedict.

"Mister Benedict, thank you so much for coming."

"The easement of your suffering is paramount to us," Benedict said.

"Where is Ms Coluthon?" For obvious reasons I could see she wasn't standing behind him.

"Turning the truck around," he said. "May I come in?"

"Of course." I stepped aside and ushered him into my hallway.

"No cutting equipment today?" I said too brightly. Benedict turned and stared up at me.

"Will it be necessary? We can bring it in, if you like."

"No, no, just a little joke." I flinched at my unfortunate choice of word and flushed red. "I've opened the office for you." I hurried over to it and pulled the heavy vault door aside. "What will you do with the desk? Once you take it away?"

"We will place it in storage, have it valued and possibly restored. We then sell it—a rare item like this should do well at auction."

"Oh, that will be nice. I hope it goes to a good home."

Benedict stepped into the vault. I thought for a moment he might be rubbing his hands together in glee, then I realised he was putting on white cotton gloves.

He started by running his hands over the panels and carved trim of the desk, then moved on to removing and examining each of the thirty-four drawers in turn, turning them over and peering at each side before slipping them back into place. He raised the desk's curved lid, sending it rattling back out of sight. With a slight grunt of effort Benedict vaulted up onto the exposed work surface. I envied the way he crawled inside the special place that I hadn't fitted into since I was a child.

On hands and knees Benedict peered and touched the interior curve of the desk's many nooks and crannies. I waited, fidgeting nervously and wondering where Drakeforth had vanished to.

"Do you own a small white dog?" Coluthon said in my ear. I jumped so hard I stumbled against a bookshelf.

"What? No. Why?"

"No reason. We moving this thing or are you going to just leave here in it, Eggs?" Coluthon pushed past me and eyed up the desk.

"It is in remarkable condition, Miss Pudding. You and your family are to be commended," Benedict said as he slid out of the desk's writing cavity and dropped to the floor.

"Thank you," I said.

"You can rest assured that this desk will trouble you no longer." He smiled kindly at me while reaching up and to pull Coluthon's hands back down to her sides as she started to mime playing a violin. Coluthon's smile flashed and soured as quickly as a bowl of rotting fruit in one of those time-lapse camera shots.

"Do you need a hand getting it out the door?" I said.

"Sure, that would be great. Tell you what, why don't you carry it out yourself while we make a cup of tea?" Coluthon replied.

"No need, best leave the removal to the experts," Benedict said.

"Are you sure?" I couldn't see it happening. The tall, toxic-tongued woman and the man who could walk under my kitchen table without knocking his head were not going to be able to carry the antique desk out themselves.

"Stand back," Benedict said. I backed into the hallway as Coluthon seized the far end of the desk and Benedict squatted at the other. He counted down from three and they lifted the desk. Benedict grasped it at the bottom, while Coluthon held her end about halfway, keeping the desk level as they shuffled across the office floor. I could see the strain they were both taking. Benedict, for all his short stature, was a ball of muscle. His arms and legs swelled like bread dough in a warm cupboard. Taking small steps, and giving each other unheeded advice, they reached the circular doorway of the office.

"How close are we!?" Coluthon shouted.

"To the door?" I asked.

"No, to the Zebredian Meridian," she snapped back.

"Door's a couple of inches…one more step," Benedict twisted his neck, and took another small step. "Right, I'm on the threshold."

Inch by inch they carried the desk out into the hallway. I remembered it had taken five men with two trolleys to move it from my parents' house and install it here when I moved in. Seeing Coluthon lose that pearlescent shine to her skin and actually sweat a little gave me a deep sense of satisfaction.

"Set her down. I need a breather." Benedict lowered his end and Coluthon set hers down a moment later. They both leaned on the desk and panted.

"Sprog it," Coluthon said, breathing deeply. "I say we leave the barnacle thing here. Set it on fire. Let the princess claim insurance and we take a cut of the pay-out."

"Except that would require burning the entire house down. Living oak is renowned for being almost fireproof," I said.

"I don't see any flaws in my suggestion," Coluthon replied levelly.

"It's worth more as it is," Benedict said, flexing his knees in a series of deep squats. "Right, sooner we get this loaded on the truck, the sooner we can break for lunch."

The desk wobbled and then levitated again, Benedict now walking forwards as Coluthon worked her way backwards towards the front door. They negotiated the front door and the three steps to street level. Coluthon had parked their covered truck across the street, blocking both lanes, with the back of it pointing at my front door. A small queue of traffic had built up on each side. The drivers were getting out and starting to demand someone move the truck. I saw Mr Haberdashery from two doors down out on the street with a leash, calling and whistling for his dog Snowflake.

Benedict and Coluthon ignored them all and manoeuvred the desk on to the truck's hydraulic loading platform. With the desk in position, Coluthon pressed a button and the platform whined up to the level of the truck's deck. Some final heaving and they vanished into the dark interior, my desk disappearing with them. For Drakeforth's plan to work, something had to happen pretty soon. He hadn't been clear on the details, but he had assured me it was fool proof. The cynic in me was awaiting the arrival of a better fool.

Coluthon emerged from the gloom of the truck's rear. I watched as she finished arranging old blankets over the desk and tying it down with cargo straps. The desk looked small and abandoned in the dark cavity of the moving truck.

Benedict rode the hydraulic platform down until he was at eye level with me. He made some final notes on a clipboard form, then handed it to me for a signature.

"We'll be in touch when we have a valuation. Our commission is fifteen per cent of either the sale or the auction price. This counts as your receipt." I nodded, tears welling up in my eyes.

"You are doing the right thing," he said, and reached out to pat me gently on the shoulder. I nodded again, wiping my eyes on my sleeve. Taking a deep breath I looked up and saw Coluthon jump down from the back of the truck. If Drakeforth didn't do something spectacular soon, the entire plan would be for nothing.

I took my copy of the invoice and agreement to sell an antique at auction. Benedict rode the loading platform to the ground. He stepped off and it folded like a duck's wing against the back of the truck.

"Have a nice day," he said and shouldered his way through the gesticulating crowd of motorists without so much as a glance above the knee at any of them.

The truck started up a few moments later, I watched as it completed a seven-point turn and ground its way out of Bugle Street.

I turned my back on the commuters berating me for delaying them and went back inside, feeling numb. I had just let the living oak desk that was the key to the entire puzzle be driven away by what I felt sure were agents of the enemy.

CHAPTER 13

Sitting in my home office, surrounded by stacks of books and papers, I stared at the indents in the carpet where the desk used to stand.

The notion that I should have explained what was going on to the desk was irrational yet hard to shake. The desk couldn't think. Empathic energy, even in living oak, was only a facsimile of life. What empathic energy engineers call anthropomorphic resonance. Our perception of and interaction with double-e flux-imbued items made them appear to behave in ways we could relate to. I felt guilt over burdening my appliances with my lack of enthusiasm every morning. It wasn't the fridge's fault that it was programmed to detect the level of preselected items and remind me when they were expired or otherwise needed replacement. If what Pretense said about my levels of empathic interaction were true, it was no wonder that everything I owned seemed to be closer to alive than even I felt most days.

I resisted the urge to go and make a cup of tea and tell the kettle how I was feeling. It might blow a heating element or something. Sighing, I stood up and waited for the wave of dizzy nausea to pass.

The rattling of the front door took me by surprise. I stumbled to it, wrenched it open and stared at the EGS Benedict and Associates moving truck parked outside.

"I told you the plan would work," Drakeforth said from my feet. I looked down.

"Drakeforth! What happened?" A dark patch of red was

spreading from his shoulder to soak the front of his shirt.

"Turns out the woman had a knife in her boot. She cut herself free while I was tying up the little guy. She slashed me quite badly. It's nothing an emergency blood transfusion, a few dozen stitches and a week in hospital won't fix."

"I'm calling you an ambulance," I said, but Drakeforth grabbed my hand.

"Please don't. If I say, okay, you'll say,, you're an ambulance and then I'll be forced to go *wee-ooo-wee-ooo* and frankly—" he broke off coughing. "Frankly, I don't have the strength for it."

"You're bleeding," I reminded him.

"No time, if we fuss about with emergency rooms and hospitals they will ask questions. The two trussed up in the back of the truck might well escape and my brilliant plan will have been for nothing."

I helped Drakeforth to his feet, half-dragging him back to the truck. With Drakeforth giving advice, seemingly at random, I got the engine started and the heavy vehicle in gear. "Drive like the wind to the Monastery of Saint Detriment," he said, slumping against the passenger side window.

Driving less like the wind and more like a sea fog, I ploughed my way through the weekday traffic and in an hour we were on the open highway.

I heard nothing from our trussed up captives in the back of the truck as I drove down the highway. I had no idea what we were meant to do with them and Drakeforth was of no help as he slipped in and out of consciousness, occasionally stirring to accuse me of writing down everything he said. Other times he would mutter odd quotations that sounded Arthurian. Night was falling when I turned off the highway and up the winding forest road that led to the monastery. By now Drakeforth had paled to the grey-green of fresh milk. He seemed to be barely breathing and the flow of blood from his wound had slowed to an oozing trickle.

"Nearly there, Drakeforth," I said loudly. The truck growled and I worked the gears, looking for something low enough to get us up the last slope.

The gates were closed and the visitors' booth unattended. Even the car park was empty. I parked the truck next to the gate, slid out and banged on the solid wood.

"Hello!?" I yelled. "I need some help out here! I have an injured man!" A full minute passed, and then I heard the rattling of chains and bolts. The smaller door set into the gate cracked open. "I'm afraid we are closed to visitors," the man on the other side began.

"We're not visitors!" I shouted. "We're travelling monks from the monastery in South Owad. We have been set upon by rabid cuttlefish. Brother Vole is badly injured." To my surprise the gate opened immediately.

I raced back to the truck and supervised Drakeforth being lifted out by a multitude of helping hands. They carried him into the courtyard under the glow of lamp light and I followed in their wake.

"Charlotte Pudding," Hoptoad said. "Your presence here poses an interesting paradox for my next meditation."

"Drakeforth has been stabbed, or cut. Either way he needs medical attention and we didn't have time to go to the hospital," I said quickly.

"Your friend is badly injured and instead of going to anyone of the fully equipped medical facilities that dot the cityscape and its satellite towns, you come all the way out here, where the best we can do is pray and perhaps put a clean bandage on it?"

"It's a long story," I admitted.

"The best ones usually are," Hoptoad replied. "We will do what we can for brother Drakeforth, for we know not how the actions we take will change us and those we act against." The monks carrying Drakeforth disappeared into the darkness, carrying him on their shoulders like brown-robed pall bearers.

"Now," said Hoptoad, "come and tell me everything."

We went to one of the common buildings where Arthurians sat and talked, drank tea or beer and read from holy texts. I sank into a soft armchair and accepted a steaming mug of walrusroot tea with a grateful smile. The air around us glowed in the light of fragrant oil lamps and racks of fat yellow candles.

"Where to start…" I said.

"You have already started," Hoptoad said. "Your choice is to now decide how you are going to shape reality by introducing me to it. It's an astonishing responsibility and one that I fear is taken all too lightly. People go rushing off telling stories without ever thinking of the effect they are going to have on their audience. Though I suppose if we thought about it too much, we'd never share anything."

"At the beginning, then?" I asked weakly.

"A good choice," Hoptoad said and sat back, a look of calm spreading across his lined face.

I told him everything, in clear detail this time. Without the hysterics or the confusing tangents. Hoptoad displayed all the best qualities of a listener: he didn't interrupt, he didn't fall asleep and he didn't make any odd sighing noises of boredom. He listened with an intensity that made me feel my story might be worth telling after all. When I was done, he straightened up and, taking a deep breath, offered me more tea.

"Will Drakeforth be okay? I should be with him. He will be furious if he wakes up and finds he has been saved by religious people."

"Odd, isn't he," Hoptoad said, showing no immediate inclination to move from his comfy chair.

"Drakeforth? Very," I agreed.

"It is odd that he opposes all that we believe so ferociously. Surely how we choose to spend our lives is little concern of his. We do not ask him to share our beliefs, or make special allowances for us. We live apart from his culture. We are self-contained and demand no tribute from him in time or material goods."

"He seems quite bothered by the Arthurians' tax-exempt status," I suggested.

"A hangover from an ancient accord. Arthurian monasteries and temples provide for society in other ways."

"Some people would say that you provide a safe environment for lunatics who would otherwise be accosting people on the streets." I'd spoken before I realised my words echoed

Drakeforth's rabidly secular sentiment. Still, it made Hoptoad chuckle.

"We have done that at times. We have also provided food, shelter and counselling for those who have nowhere else to go. The most important thing we offer to anyone who has the strength to believe is the chance to become one with a higher power, to plumb the great mysteries of the universe."

"From where I'm sitting the chances of becoming one with a higher power seem very slim. It's all right for you, you've spent thirty years growing your beard and making herbal remedies."

"If I shave my beard and cut what remains of my hair, I would still be at peace with Arthur," Hoptoad replied.

"If what you believe was actually true, wouldn't everyone be doing it? Wouldn't it be so blindingly obvious we would all be wearing beards, robes and living the monastic lifestyle?"

"There are none so blind as those that cannot see." Hoptoad quoted the words of Arthur that were displayed on one of the signs outside the gate.

"That's like saying, there are none so able to come dead last in a hundred yard swimming race as those with no arms and legs."

"Exactly," Hoptoad smiled and nodded. "You have the makings of a fine Master of Art."

"I hardly think so. Don't you need to be a special kind of person to attain that level in Arthurianism?"

"A master is merely someone who started doing something before you," Hoptoad said.

"I'm sure Drakeforth would say that also applies to those who simply suffered some kind of mental breakdown earlier."

"You place a lot of stock in what Drakeforth says, or what you imagine he would say. Yet you speak very little of what you believe."

"I guess that's because so much of what Drakeforth says is beginning to make sense. Personally, I would like to embrace the certain belief that there is more to life than the simple biological urge to reproduce. I would like to believe in a higher power. I would like to feel that I could suspend my credulity and embrace something as simple and reassuring as Arthurianism. Except, I have personal experience of how completely indifferent the universe is. Wishing it were different won't change the facts." I stopped speaking and breathed. The anger that Drakeforth so cheerfully wore on his sleeve now threatened to burst out of my carefully tended calm facade.

"It would change how you experience the facts. How you respond to them, and how you enjoy your passage through what we so naively perceive as time and space," Hoptoad said.

I stood up, "I would like to check on Drakeforth now, please."

Hoptoad stood with me. "Of course."

We left the snug confines of the lounge and went out under the dark vault of the night sky. The view through the clean country air was brighter than in the city, where light pollution reduced the sparkle of the stars. I found myself staring upwards, trying, in vain as always, to count the uncountable and to put some comprehension around the infinite.

"Blows your mind, doesn't it?" Hoptoad said, his face also tilted upwards. "When I try to get my head around just how utterly infinite we can be I get an ice-cream headache. It is written that when Saint Diestock came unto his Revelation of the Pumpernickel the grandeur of it so overwhelmed him that he collapsed and died."

"Or maybe he died of something like a stroke or a heart attack and never had a revelation?" I said, turning slowly and watching the galaxy spin before my eyes.

"His disciple, the Offer of Bob, heard his dying breath. The sacred utterance was quite clear."

I didn't reply, instead I drew my sense of wonder back into its physical shell and returned my gaze to the more easily comprehended ground beneath my feet.

The monks of Arthur tended the sick, the injured and the insane in a low-roofed building beyond the vegetable gardens. The hospital with its whitewashed bricks and clay tile roof followed the concave curve of the monastery's outer wall. We entered through a round door; the smell of antiseptics and incense mixed in the air like anchovies and chocolate. Oil lamps glowed with warm light at regular intervals along the walls.

Hoptoad washed his hands at a sink near the door. I followed suit and we went down the aisle between two rows of beds. Very few of the patients were Arthurians; most looked lost and wretched, the people equivalent of abandoned puppies. I saw Drakeforth perched on the edge of a bed, shirtless, his shoulder now clean and bandaged. He gesticulated with his good arm at a slim, bearded woman who rocked slightly on the balls of her feet, hands clasped behind her back, while Drakeforth lectured at her.

"Once again, Doctor Primum, you are relying on the ancient reports of a barely literate food taster to qualify your entire existence. There is no way she could have theorised the existence of alternate universes by regarding bowls of steamed vegetables."

"We do not ask the essential elements of existence why they deliver revelations unto us. We simply seek to understand the revelations received by those lucky enough to be in the right place at the moment of correct perception," the woman replied.

"Suggesting Saint Birthoot conceived the theory of transition between high-energy states of sub-atomic particles by simply looking at the random patterns in a plate of peas and corn is ludicrous!"

"And yet, that is what happened." The sister remained placid in the face of Drakeforth's apoplexy.

"You are all complete and utter morons!" Drakeforth announced.

"I am pleased to see you are feeling better, Drakeforth," I said hurriedly, stepping between them.

"Please, get me out of this madhouse," he said petulantly.

"I recommend you stay the night," the sister said. "You lost a lot of blood, and there is still the risk of infection."

"Why don't you pray to Arthur to heal me?" Drakeforth said with all the acid of a sour candy.

"I trust Arthur to guide me to make the right use of my medical degree," the doctor replied. "In Arthur's second Telling, the Synopsis of the Creation, he teaches us that he had little time for cooks who spit in their own food."

The doctor took a hypodermic syringe and injected a shot of

something into Drakeforth's arm.

"This should help dull the pain," she said with a slight smile.

"Help me with my shirt, Pudding." Drakeforth extended his good arm and I helped him dress in a clean cotton shirt the Arthurians had provided. A young monk hurried in to the ward and drew Hoptoad aside, whispering urgently in the old man's ear.

The doctor addressed us both. "You should have the dressing changed in a couple of days. The stitches will need to come out in about a week. If you become feverish, the wound begins to bleed, seep or smell bad, seek medical attention immediately."

"One last thing before you go," said Hoptoad, returning to the conversation. "The monastery is surrounded by Godden Energy Corporation agents."

"What?" I said.

"I can only imagine that they feel they have not made their position clear to you previously," he continued.

"I think Pretense made his point quite succinctly." I buttoned up Drakeforth's shirt.

"Is there another way out of here?" Drakeforth asked as he worked his feet into his blood-splattered shoes.

"Of course, but to use it you would need to spend a life time in contemplation and fine-tune your consciousness to the rhythm of the celestial song," Hoptoad said.

"In the next two minutes?" Drakeforth asked.

"We can offer you sanctuary," Hoptoad suggested.

"That would be great, thank you," I said.

"We'll get you dressed in proper attire and then hide you among the faithful." Hoptoad sent the young monk off into the darkness and we hurried out of the ward and across the courtyard.

I could hear the throbbing of helicopters overhead and see the golden fingers of their searchlights pointing at the trees and hills outside the monastery. We moved along the wall, passing the gardens and the pens where animals grunted, snorted, and watched us with yellow eyes.

In the sermon hall, which Hoptoad called the Collider,

because it was a place where ideas and people came together, we changed into the garb of the initiated. Donning wigs, false beards and brown robes, we blended into the throng of people now moving into the chamber and taking their positions around the spiral pattern in the floor. Hundreds of candles flickered in a refreshing draught that was flowing in through the open door, the light reflecting off the patchouli-polished wooden floor.

"*The desk*," I whispered, turning to Drakeforth in horror.

"Has been rescued," Hoptoad said calmly. "It is hidden in the herbarium."

"Okay…" I didn't have time to ask what the herbarium was and why it might be a good place to hide the living oak desk. Another thought struck me.

"And, um…the other things in the back of the truck?"

"They seemed overtly angry, so we left them tied up," Hoptoad said.

"Is this a normal meeting?" Drakeforth's eyes were soft and dazed.

"No meeting of the faithful is normal. We are all extraordinary," Hoptoad said.

"The floor is on fire," Drakeforth said. I looked down. Hoptoad seemed unperturbed.

"Doctor Primum may have given him too much," the monk explained.

"Too much? Too much what?"

"I'm not exactly sure. It's a herbal medicine. We use it as a painkiller and an antiseptic. It has some fascinating side effects."

"Is it safe?" I watched with macabre fascination as Drakeforth lifted the fronds of his flowing beard and let them drift from his fingers.

"Quite safe. Though he should not drive for several hours."

With Hoptoad's help, I got Drakeforth kneeling among the other worshippers. Hoptoad left us to move around the spiral, walking ever closer to the central point.

Once there he turned in a full circle and greeted with the congregation as he had done in our first visit. "I am with us. I am within all of us. I am the clothes we wear. The food we eat. The water we drink. I am all of us. I was, I am and I will be."

The door to the collider burst open and armed agents of Godden came jogging in, splitting off and taking up positions around the wall.

CHAPTER 14

Hoptoad continued his sermon, ignoring the interruption. The congregation regarded the new arrivals with interest and when the black-suited guards did nothing beyond moving into position around the chamber walls, they turned their attention back to Hoptoad.

I kept my head down, afraid that even under the disguise of wig and beard, someone might recognise me. Not that I recognised any of them. They all wore the same black uniform; even their faces looked cast from the same small set of genetic dice.

"We are aware," an agent's voice echoed around the collider hall, "that there are two among you whom we seek. They will be found. The future cannot be stopped."

Hoptoad's gaze dropped to the floor. "Thank you for joining us. The future is concurrent with the present and the past. We accept that all things are happening simultaneously."

"Everyone will stand, everyone will be examined," the agent announced. We dutifully rose to our feet in silence. None of the Arthurians seemed at all outraged or even mildly concerned by the invasion. To my left, Drakeforth started giggling.

The agents moved down the line of the faithful, tugging on beards. This elicited a grunt from the men whose facial hair was a natural feature and a patient arch of the eyebrows from the women who wore their beards on elastic strings. I watched with growing unease as they worked their way towards us. The Collider hall was silent, except for the ping-snap of elastic cord and Drakeforth's barely contained snort-giggles.

I tensed, ready to bolt, to grab Drakeforth and run. It didn't matter where, or how far we would get. The important thing was to not just stand here and wait for the inevitable discovery. I reached out and took Drakeforth's arm as the Goddens advanced down the line towards us.

"I get it," Drakeforth announced. I stared at him in shock. He was going to get us caught for sure. Drakeforth pushed his way forward, passing between the spiral rows of Arthurians towards Hoptoad.

"In fact I get it so much I have something to say." Drakeforth reached the centre of the chamber. The agents of Godden paused in their search and watched him.

"I am Arthur," Drakeforth said.

"I am all of us. I was, I am and I will be," Hoptoad intoned.

"Yes, yes," Drakeforth waved a dismissive hand. "I'm Arthur," he said again.

"That is an interesting claim," Hoptoad said.

"It's the only answer that makes any sense," Drakeforth replied.

"Can you prove it?" said one of the faithful from the curving spiral of the assembled.

"If you require proof, you lack the faith required to accept the truth and are not ready to have the truth revealed to you," Drakeforth said. The gathered worshippers began to murmur, discussing this point with their neighbours.

"It is said Arthur shall return to us in the form of a wheel of cheese!" another dissident called out from the back.

"No, he shall appear in the mathematics of the perfect equation!" someone else countered.

"A sunflower!"

"A thought shared by all those who believe at the same instant!"

"A flock of talking gnats!"

"A whisper!"

"A shout!"

"A giant burning moose!"

The voices came from all points of the room, everyone calling out what they felt to be the truth of the return of Arthur. His cryptic Tellings had been interpreted and defined over the centuries and it seemed that no one had ever come to the same conclusion.

They fell to arguing; voices were raised and hands too. Drakeforth stood in the centre of this maelstrom. Hoptoad, waiting with his usual impassive calm, stood beside him.

"I am Arthur," Drakeforth repeated, his voice booming from the sweet spot in the chamber's carefully designed acoustics to smother the fire of dogmatic debate flaring around him.

"When will we ascend?" someone cried.

"What lies beyond this perception?" someone else asked.

"Why can we not know a sub-atomic particle's position and its direction of travel at the same time?"

Drakeforth raised his hands, and the roar of voices faded.

"It's really not that important," he declared. The room fell into absolute silence for several heartbeats, and then with a roar the crowd surged forward. Angry voices shouted and the commands of the agents of Godden were lost in the cacophony. I struggled against the flood of people, lost my footing and was swept along in the crush of the mob. I heard shouts, screams and the rip of Drakeforth's robes being shredded by the suddenly offended devotees of the Art.

What happened next felt like a puff of wind and a push by a giant hand. The air shimmered and we flew backwards, sliding across the polished floor like brown-robed hockey pucks.

Only Drakeforth remained, stripped to his underwear, the bandage on his shoulder wound torn away, the skin underneath bruised but cleanly stitched.

"Naughty," he warned. The Arthurians collected themselves. There were no more angry shouts or demands for answers. They stared at Drakeforth and then slowly, in ones and twos, began to kneel at the points around the spiral, waiting for him to share his all-encompassing wisdom. I stood alone in stunned surprise.

"Are you seriously telling us that you are a god?" I called over the heads of the faithful.

"Of course not. Gods don't exist," Drakeforth called back. "I never expected anyone to take what I said seriously. Mostly it was just made up."

"Made up? Made up? What in the highbrow helix were you making up such confusing twaddle for?" I lifted the hem of my robe and marched through the kneeling crowd.

"To impress girls, mostly. They love a guy who sounds profound," Drakeforth said with a shrug.

"An entire religion exists around everything Arthur is supposed to have said! Now you turn up, reveal yourself to the faithful and say, sorry you bunch of charcoal briquettes, but you've got it all wrong?"

"Well..." Drakeforth began.

"The answer to one of the most important philosophical questions in history. The debate that has cost thousands of lives, changed the course of history over fifteen centuries and caused the indoctrination of entire cultures and it was all so you could pick up chicks?" I asked, incredulous.

"I wouldn't put it quite that way," he said.

"Arthurianism has answered a lot of questions for a lot of people. It has led many of them to live long, peaceful and ultimately fulfilled lives," Hoptoad said.

"You cannot be taking this seriously?" I asked Hoptoad.

"Arthur was, is and shall be. We observe and by doing so shape reality. Arthur is among us," the old monk said.

"You complete bunch of grass-chewers," I said. "Why does a guy announcing himself as Arthur returned make any difference?"

"No one has ever made that declaration before," Hoptoad said. "Only Arthur himself would claim to be Arthur returned. Therefore, he is."

"Fine! I'm Arthur! I am among you!" I raised my arms and turned to face the crowd.

"Now you're just being silly," Hoptoad chided.

"Those are the two we want," an agent declared. "Seize them." The strangely identical agents of Godden stepped forward.

"And just how are you going to get us out of this situation,

Arthur?" I asked, backing away from the advancing agents.

The Arthurians stood and moved together, until they stood shoulder to shoulder, each blocking the advance. "Hold on to yourselves," Hoptoad said. I opened my mouth to ask why when the floor under my feet vanished. We dropped like three stones, my fake beard flying up and obscuring the view. I hit my head on something hard, the stars flared briefly and I passed out.

CHAPTER 15

"Ouch," summed up my feelings perfectly. "Ouch," I said again and tried to sit up. Sometime later consciousness returned for a second attempt.

"Easy does it," Drakeforth said. His hands guided me into a sitting position. "Here, drink this." The warm liquid smelled like tea, but tasted of mint and citrus essence. I felt better after each sip.

"What happened?" I asked, taking in the oddly clinical room. Each surface had the silver sheen of surgical steel. A row of gurneys lay empty, except for the one I was sitting on. "Am I in hospital?"

"Not quite," Hoptoad said, coming into view.

"You aren't going to believe what this place is," Drakeforth said. I noticed he was dressed in monks' robes again. Like me, he had lost the wig and beard.

"It's not the afterlife?" I asked.

"Almost," Drakeforth grinned. "We should get moving. It won't be long before the Goddens work out how to get to us."

I made it to my feet with minimal assistance. The room swayed slightly, but I felt no worse than I usually did. We left the silver room with its empty gurneys through a pair of swinging doors. The next room contained a single bed-sized platform with a cushioned headrest under what looked like a large telescope, the end of which vanished into a spaghetti network of pipes and ducts in the ceiling.

"And that is?" I left the question hanging.

"A long story," Hoptoad replied. The lights here were empathically powered. They came on as we walked and glowed down on us with genuine warmth.

"Wait, Arthurians don't use empathic technology." I squinted at the shining globes in the ceiling.

"A very long story," Hoptoad clarified. "We really should hurry." He exited the room through a second set of doors. We almost jogged down a short, metal-lined hallway, my head pounding harder with each step. Another set of swinging doors and we found ourselves on the edge of a concrete-floored loading bay. The fresh night air blowing in through the open doorway helped ease the drumbeat in my skull.

"This is as far as I can take you," Hoptoad said. "The road to the monastery is at the end of this trail. Be sure to turn left at the first intersection. Miss Pudding, you can make your own way down to the highway from there. Oh and please, take this with my compliments, a reminder of our perception of the time we have shared." He handed me a jar of goosefat marmalade.

"What about Drakeforth?" I asked, taking the jar and discovering I didn't have any pockets in my Arthurian robe.

"The Lord Arthur will stay here, of course. We have so much to discuss. So much for him to explain and clarify. I fear it may take more time than I have in my life to work through it all."

"You can't be serious?" I asked.

"Of course he is serious," Drakeforth said. "Hoptoad, my most deluded and faithful servant. I need you to do something for me."

"Of course, Arthur," Hoptoad bowed slightly, his beard tips sweeping the concrete floor.

"Continue the great work you are doing," Drakeforth said. "Share the ancient wisdom of my Tellings with all those who come seeking it. Continue to grow prize-winning vegetables, free-range livestock and herbs both culinary and medicinal. Embrace the past, present and future, for they are all happening simultaneously."

"Of course," Hoptoad dipped again. "With your guidance—"

"Arthur is retiring," Drakeforth interrupted. "You guys will have to work it out on your own. Just as you have done for the last fifteen centuries."

"I...oh...as you command, Arthur," Hoptoad said. Frowning, he turned to go back the way we had come.

"Hoptoad," I called after him.

"Yes?" he said with a guilty start.

"Would it not make more sense for us to hide out down here until the GEC have gone? Then we can use the patchouli oil on the desk to find out why they want it so badly?"

"Faith tends to shy away from closer inspection. By its very definition, faith requires the suspension of empirical evidence. Arthurians are fortunate in that we have a great deal of empirical and theoretical evidence to support our faith. Which means, we don't actually have any faith in our belief system. What we have is knowledge, and knowledge can be a very dangerous thing." Hoptoad half-waved and started towards the swinging doors that led back inside.

"What has that got to do with anything?" I asked, stepping after him.

Hoptoad stopped and sighed. "In summary, the greater the distance between you and the desk, the less knowledge you will have and the safer we will all be."

"But we brought it here to discover its secret. With patchouli oil," I reminded him.

"It would be better for everyone if the desk was broken up and its individual parts burned," Hoptoad said with a sorrowful expression.

"You cannot be serious?" I would have laughed, but Hoptoad's face was grim.

"Go home, Miss Pudding. You have brought the desk here. We Arthurians alone can accept the responsibility of understanding, as we have always done."

I looked to Drakeforth for support, but he appeared to be fascinated with the way his hands moved and wasn't paying attention to the conversation at all.

"I will be back for that desk! I will find out the truth!" I realised I sounded like Drakeforth when he was in a rant. I shot him a glance and was dismayed to see that he had pinched his lips between two fingers and was now stretching them out to peer at them down his nose.

Hoptoad walked away, leaving us standing in the cool, pine-scented air.

"We should get started," I said. "It's a long walk to the highway." I started across the loading bay towards the open doors.

Drakeforth released his face. "We aren't going to walk. We are going to ride."

I looked around. The empty loading bay had room, I guessed, for no more than a pair of trucks. It seemed this was where the monastery took delivery of the few essential supplies they couldn't make themselves. The only odd thing I could see were the large steel tanks off to one side.

"What are you seeing that I'm not?" I asked.

Drakeforth started violently, one arm swinging in a wide arc before settling in a point at the steel tanks. "The pressure gauges on those tanks are showing they are at capacity," he declared.

"Yes," I nodded.

He executed another stumbling half turn. "The clipboard manifest hanging on the wall behind us shows that they are emptied at the same time every month."

"It does?" I turned to look.

"And…" Drakeforth let the weight of a dramatic pause build, "Hoptoad told me that the tanker truck would be here any minute."

"You really are Arthur returned," I said dryly. We took up a position inside the hallway doors at the back of the loading bay. A few minutes passed in uncomfortable silence while I racked my brain for ideas on how to get the desk back and secure a sufficient quantity of patchouli oil without being noticed by either the Arthurians or the Godden Energy Corporation. My mental design of a complex operation involving helium balloons, a croquet team and a dozen orange-glazed hams was interrupted as the headlights of a truck filled the loading bay.

We peered through the doors as the tanker turned around and

backed in. A man in fastidiously clean white overalls jumped from the cab. He unfastened a heavy hose from underneath the truck chassis, carried it over to the closest tank and twisted it into a pump socket. We heard the hissing rush of something transferring as the pipe swelled and twitched with the pressure of the flow.

"Go," Drakeforth whispered. We slipped through the doors. Crouching low, we scuttled around the other side of the truck. I reached up and opened the cab door. Seeing it was clear, I climbed up and slid over to the driver's seat. Drakeforth clambered up after me.

"Let's go," he whispered.

"Wait…" I hunkered down and watched the driver in the side mirror. He closed the tank valve and unscrewed the connection. I waited for him to finish stowing the hose back under the truck before I pressed the starter. The engine shuddered and hummed into life.

"Oi!" the driver shouted. We ignored him and a moment later the truck rolled out into the turning area outside.

"Hoptoad said the painkillers they gave me have some side effects."

"You seem to be doing okay," I replied, my focus on the narrow road.

Drakeforth gave me a puzzled look. "I was talking to the camel."

I fastened my seatbelt as we picked up speed and soon enough we reached the intersection. I remembered Hoptoad's instructions: left to head down the monastery road towards the highway, right to go back up the hill to the monastery. I stopped.

"Left!" Drakeforth blurted, looking in the side mirror for signs of pursuit.

"The little man and the blonde with a knife, they're still tied up in the back of the moving truck," I said.

"And?" Drakeforth asked, clearly feeling no sympathy for either of them.

"They might be in danger. Who knows what the agents of Godden will do to them." I hesitated for another second.

"If they are in fact in the employ of Godden, then I expect they will be given a cup of tea and authorisation to shoot us on sight," Drakeforth said.

"Imagine never knowing for sure," I said, the truck vibrating beneath us without moving.

"Imagine regretting your decision to find out for the brief time we are incarcerated by Pretense before the desk is destroyed or locked up forever." Drakeforth seemed to be sobering up.

"Knowledge is our greatest weapon," I said, twisting the steering wheel and sending the truck lumbering up the hill.

"I'd rather come back with something more gun-like in our arsenal."

I ignored Drakeforth and we drove through the night, up the winding hill road, through the whispering pine trees until the buzzing of helicopters told us we were close.

"Happy now?" he asked.

"Ecstatic," I replied, leaning forward and peering through the windscreen at the scene before us.

Benedict's truck stood where we left it. Benedict himself stood to one side, giving orders, judging by the way he was waving his hands about. Coluthon stood back, puffing on her pipe and watching as agents of Godden carried my desk out of the monastery gate and loaded it into the back of the truck.

"Pan-fried posteriors," Drakeforth swore. "Now what are we going to do?"

"Turn this tanker around, and see where they're going." I launched into a complicated series of rotating manoeuvres. The heavily laden tanker truck turned its back on the monastery a few degrees at a time. We were nearly on our way when one of the agents approached us.

"Trouble," Drakeforth warned. I grabbed a greasy bounceball cap from the seat beside me and pulled it down over my eyes before winding down the window.

"Wotcher," I said gruffly.

"What are you doing here?" the agent said.

"First time out here. I got lost making the pickup. Sorted now," I said.

"Do you know where you are going?" the agent asked.

"Uhh…"

"Return to the highway. We will escort you to the delivery point from there." He marched back up the hill without waiting for a response.

"That was interesting," I said, winding the window back up and giving Drakeforth a reassuring grin.

"Godden," Drakeforth said.

"No, just one of his agents," I replied.

"The logo on your cap. This is a Godden Energy Corporation truck."

I yanked the hat off and looked at it. The heart and lightning bolt logo of Energy Tech Services was embroidered on the front.

"What the haemorrhoid is going on?" I demanded.

"It's worse than I suspected," Drakeforth said as I engaged the gears and sent the truck chugging down the hill road.

"We'll have to go deeper into the darkness, Pudding, a lot deeper than we might like. There'll be barked shins on the unseen furniture of this mystery before we are done. Mark my words."

We reached the highway without incident. "We find out where they are going, then we can strike from within and get my desk back," I explained.

"We can't stop now," Drakeforth said. "This isn't some sense-media adventure where you can disconnect and return to your dull and dreary life. This is it. This is you, living, making the big decisions and taking the big risks."

"Does it bother you that even if we succeed, very few will ever know? Certainly no one will if we fail," I asked.

"No reason not to try," Drakeforth said, watching the side mirror as the cab filled with light from the convoy coming down from the monastery.

We pulled out behind Benedict's truck and drove quietly down the highway. I stopped talking to Drakeforth, instead sinking into my own thoughts for the duration. It took an hour for the convoy to reach the turn-off that lead to the mysterious place that the Godden agent had called Nowhere. Going to our certain doom by helicopter had been much quicker.

CHAPTER 16

The same gate guard as before cheerfully waved us through and into the vast storage yard of the Godden base. I had pulled on the bounceball cap again. Drakeforth dug around in the glove compartment and found a pair of oversized sunglasses with fluorescent orange frames. He put them on, and turned to look at me.

"Ah, no. You are aware that wearing those will attract more attention than no disguise at all?" I asked. Drakeforth gave a wounded shrug and put the glasses away again.

An agent in a bright green fluoro safety vest directed us to a pumping station. The concrete parking slab and large intake pipe with connecting nozzle were a match for the one back at the Monastery of Saint Detriment.

"I suppose we should unload. No point in arousing suspicion," I said. Drakeforth agreed and we both climbed down and heaved the hose out from under the truck. Struggling under the ungainly weight, we dragged it over to the nozzle.

"I think you push it in and then twist that ring," I said, my arms full of anaconda pipe.

"Right." We shuffled forward, bringing the two ends together. Drakeforth reached out and spun the ring on the nozzle, locking the hose in place.

"There should be a valve lever at your end somewhere," I said. It took him a moment to find it. Drakeforth turned it to OPEN and the pipe inflated with a hiss. Bright lights and sparks immediately burst out of the ring where the hose joined the pipe. An explosion of cold fireworks in a shimmering rainbow of colours lit up Drakeforth's startled expression.

"Shut it off! Shut it off!" I yelled. He twisted the valve shut and the light show faded.

"Empathic energy," I said, hurrying over.

"The Arthurians are harvesting double-e flux from somewhere and supplying it to the Godden Energy Corporation," Drakeforth agreed.

"Where are the Arthurians getting it from?"

"Maybe they're growing living oak somewhere in those hills?" I knew it shouldn't be possible, but where else would so much empathic energy be coming from?

Drakeforth tightened the connecting ring on the hose. "Open the valve again, we'll head inside and see if we can find the desk."

I twisted the valve open; the hose swelled again and the double-e flux drained from the truck's tank. We abandoned the vehicle and went to find a way inside.

A guard stood watchful and alert outside the first door we found. We hunkered down behind a pallet and took stock.

"You go and seduce him, I'll wait here," Drakeforth said.

"Why don't you go over there and seduce him," I retorted.

"Because if he is not that way inclined, then it will be very awkward," Drakeforth explained.

"Can we distract him instead?" I suggested.

"If having a woman wearing Arthurian robes popping up out of nowhere and attempting to seduce him while on he's on duty doesn't distract him, I think we could safely declare him clinically dead."

"He looks oddly familiar," I said, my eyes squinting to focus in the dim light.

"Well, if you think you know him, try that tack. Remember, distract him and then I'll knock him out." Drakeforth gave me a shove and I stumbled out from behind the barrels. Caught like the proverbial jellyfish in a hydrophone I straightened up and walked confidently towards the guard, who immediately regarded me with suspicion, his pacifier truncheon moving to a strike position.

"Hi," I said.

"Who are you and what are you doing here?" the guard asked.

"Charlotte, and to be honest, I have no idea. It's all rather complicated."

"Don't move, I'm contacting my superior," the guard replied.

I tried to remember a good seduction technique, but as I wasn't wearing anything remotely sexy, or in possession of a bar tab credit, I drew a blank. As the guard lifted a radio from his belt I lunged forward and to the great surprise of both of us, I kissed him firmly on the mouth.

After a moment the guard jerked his head forward and butted me in the nose.

I yelped and stumbled back, clutching my face. The guard was also gripping his head and dancing around as Drakeforth hopped about behind him, a steel bar in his hands.

"Ow! Ow! Ow! Nggghhh! That really stings!" The guard hissed through clenched teeth.

"You were supposed to knock him out," I snapped in a loud whisper.

"Do you know how hard it is to render someone unconscious without killing them or causing long-term brain damage?" Drakeforth snapped back.

"Actually? No, I have no idea how challenging it can be to knock someone out. Because I've never been in a situation where it was necessary before!"

"Am I bleeding?" the guard asked, probing the back of his skull and then peering at his fingertips.

"I don't think so. Here, let me see." I gently touched the back of his head. A hard lump was rising and I wondered if he might have a concussion.

"Yes, just a little. But bumps on the head always bleed a lot, don't they? Are you feeling dizzy? Seeing double? Or..." I struggled to remember what other symptoms might indicate concussion. "Or hearing the ocean?" I peered into the guard's face with concern.

"What the handkerchief were you thinking?" the guard demanded of Drakeforth. "You could have killed me."

"I'm sure you will be fine," I said quickly. "But perhaps you should report to the med-bay for a proper check-up?"

"That really, really hurt," the guard pressed the point.

"Well, thank you for your participation in this training exercise," Drakeforth said. "Please proceed to the medical station for treatment and evaluation."

The guard scowled at us and started to walk away. I could hear him muttering about unsafe working conditions as he disappeared among the stacked containers.

"Excellent seduction technique," Drakeforth congratulated me. He dropped the bar and tried the door. It opened and the noise of a busy factory rushed out to meet us.

We stood just inside the factory entrance. Ahead of us was a hive of activity where every bee was focused on making more bees.

The workshop was the size of a zipillen hangar. Assembly lines of body parts passed overhead. Ranks of artificial people attached legs, arms and heads to torsos that walked off to join their creators at the assembly line. The assembly process was completed by these artificial people being worked on and working on the factory floor, so we were entirely ignored.

We walked like we knew where we were going. I nudged Drakeforth and indicated an unmarked door. It wasn't locked, which fitted our façade of confidence perfectly. On the other side we found a hallway lined with fake pot plants. Abstract art prints hung on the walls, overlooking a patterned carpet that pushed the limits of taste and Euclidian geometry.

"Wow," Drakeforth said staring at the floor.

"It's easier if you just don't look at it," I suggested.

"Is the carpet talking to you, too?"

"Uhh. No," I said.

"Okay then," Drakeforth lifted his eyes, set his shoulders back and marched off down the corridor. We had a purpose here: find the desk and get out. Alive.

Drakeforth and I took turns opening doors. Most of them

revealed empty offices, and store rooms of cartons stacked on wooden pallets. When we came across a set of bathrooms we both looked at each other wordlessly, went in the respective doors and emerged a few minutes later feeling relieved.

After twenty minutes searching we agreed that the desk wasn't on this floor. While the elevators weren't the safest option when we were trying to find the desk without being detected, their convenience was alluring, so we pushed the button and waited for it to arrive like a couple of employees.

"Which floor?" Drakeforth asked, staring at the banks of unlit buttons inside.

"Is there one labelled 'stolen desk storage'?"

"Yes, but that would be too obvious, wouldn't it?"

I found myself actually looking to see if he was kidding, but of course he was. I covered by punching Drakeforth lightly in the arm.

"Favourite number?" Drakeforth asked.

"Seven," I said automatically. I just like the way it sounds. He pushed the button for the seventh floor and we waited while the lift hummed. Our chosen floor turned out to contain more empty offices and a conference room filled with dusty holiday decorations and a bunch of mostly deflated balloons, now as withered and unpleasant as puffball fungi.

"No one has been here in ages," I said.

"Not quite true." Drakeforth indicated a trail of trolley tracks in the dusty carpet. They ended at a bookshelf filled with such titles as *Mangar's Management Matrix*, *A Biographers Guide to the Armistice Agenda*, and *A Journey Through the Carpal Tunnel and Other Engineering Marvels*.

"There must be some kind of switch or lever," Drakeforth mused while running his hands over the spines of the books.

I stared at the shelf for a moment and then reached out and pulled the obvious one. The bookshelf clicked and swung slightly outward on hidden hinges.

"*Open Sauce: a Collaborative Collection of Shared Recipes for Tasty Condiments, Gravies and Jus,*" I said.

"Lucky guess," Drakeforth suggested. I gave a half shrug.

Choosing the seventh floor had been a lucky guess. Selecting the right book to open the hidden doorway on my first attempt was more like luring luck into a dark alleyway and mugging it.

"You should consider becoming a burglar," Drakeforth said. I hesitated with one hand poised to pull the secret door open.

"Is it burglary if we are simply stealing back what was mine to begin with?"

"I'm hardly qualified to give you legal advice, but on the face of it, I would say if we are caught, you will be in a lot of trouble."

"Me? You're in this up to your perfectly arched eyebrows too, Drakeforth."

"You have the most endearing indignant squeak," he said and together we opened the bookshelf.

On the other side we found a safe room, one of those places where rich people can lock themselves away with enough food, water and recorded television to last until the invaders have left or the newspapers have moved on to a new scandal.

The room was packed with old furniture under shrouds of clear plastic. We moved among antique tables, chairs and a collection of iron bedheads. Drakeforth bent to examine these more closely. "Rout iron," he announced.

I dreaded asking. "Rout iron?"

"So named because it is shaped from the discarded armaments left by an army fleeing the battlefield."

As usual I found it impossible to be sure if Drakeforth was serious or if his sense of humour was so highly pitched only dogs could hear it.

I ran my hand over a covered chair. The shroud was clean. The deep-pile carpet on the floor had been vacuumed, too. In fact there was no dust on any of the plastic covers or surfaces.

"Why is this room so clean?" I asked.

"Perhaps the furniture is being stored until it is needed?" Drakeforth suggested.

"Well, the dust covers would make sense, then," I said.

"Unlike this quite frankly disturbing album of wedding lithographs," Drakeforth said, holding up a white leather-bound book with thick pages that creaked when turned.

Each dark image showed an older gentlemen standing stiffly in the thankfully short-lived fashion of Mascotalia, where the fashion-conscious wore anthropomorphic animal costumes. At his elbow, on a raised wooden pedestal, stood a small fruit bat wearing a tiny white wedding dress and lacy head piece, complete with veil.

"Mr and Mrs Huddy Godden," I said in an awed whisper.

"How do you think they consummated their marriage?" Drakeforth asked with morbid fascination.

"I'd rather not think about it."

"Too late!" Drakeforth grinned and slammed the album shut with a thud.

We moved past more furniture, trunks of books and mouldering papers, a set of kitchen scissors mounted in a glass-fronted case and a mummified sandwich, vacuum sealed in a plastic bag. The bread had turned black with age and the thin, desiccated wagon-wheel shape of what might once have been a slice of tomato stuck out from between the two stone-like slabs.

"Hungry?" Drakeforth said with a grin that I ignored.

"It's like a museum," I said with a sudden thought. "Or at least a store room for items that will go in a museum."

"I don't see your desk anywhere," Drakeforth replied.

I closed my eyes. The desk was close; I could feel it. My skin tingled with the memory of touching the smooth polished slats. "There," I said, pointing and beginning to walk before I even opened my eyes. We moved an empty bookshelf, a fruit bowl with some shrivelled apple cores in it and an almost life-size portrait of a younger Huddy Godden, and there it was—my desk—covered in heavy plastic sheeting and trussed up with tape like a Hibernal feast turkey.

"Help me get the plastic off," I said, plucking at the tape.

"Or we could leave it safely wrapped up until we get it back to the Monastery of Saint Detriment," Drakeforth countered.

"It looks like it's suffocating." I wanted to touch the desk again, to reassure the drawers that I had not abandoned them.

"It's a desk, Pudding. It does not breathe."

Part of me wanted to object. Of course it breathed. The desk snored gently in the warm afternoon sun. It snorted and coughed when I disturbed it. I managed to get the sticky tape off the plastic sheet and with a cacophony of crackling I pulled the cover aside.

"Hello, desk," I said fondly.

"Perhaps it did suffocate and it's now dead?" Drakeforth said when there was no response.

"Don't be crass," I said. Running my hands over the roll top I patted it gently. "You remember Drakeforth. I'm afraid he can be a bit of a tool," I said to the desk.

"By which she means I am indispensable, and very useful in a range of situations," Drakeforth said. "Can we go now?"

"Help me clear the way." I started moving furniture and boxes aside. The desk had been left on a wheeled trolley. I felt confident that once we cleared a path, I could push it all the way to the elevator myself.

"While I am sure your plan is brilliant, could you possibly share the main points with me? I'm interested in knowing what role you see for me in our daring escape," Drakeforth said.

I stopped pushing the desk trolley. *Escape plan?*

"Bratwurst," I muttered. "I honestly hadn't thought that far ahead."

"Well then," Drakeforth straightened up and dusted his hands off. "Perhaps we should just give ourselves up now?"

"No." I started pushing the trolley again. "If we quit now and later on realise that things could have got an awful lot worse, we'll kick ourselves for giving up when things were going quite well."

Drakeforth pondered my reasoning for a moment and must have found it sound. He put his back into it and we kept the trolley rolling through the meadow-like carpet.

The final gap was narrow, but it was enough. I was panting by the time we reached the back of the bookshelf door.

"Well. Open it," I wheezed at Drakeforth.

"I can't," he said, hands pressing against the smooth wooden surface. "There's no handle on this side."

CHAPTER 17

waited for Drakeforth to laugh, to grin, to remind me that his cutting sarcasm was part of his charm. Instead he scrabbled to get his fingers in the crack between door and wall.

"Really?" I said, still unsure.

"No, I just thought it would be more fun to dig my way out using my fingernails." Drakeforth sounded tense.

"Okay," I said and took a deep breath. "This is what we are going to do." I didn't feel concerned that I was speaking to Drakeforth as though he were one of my clients who couldn't get their printer drivers to install properly. "Step back, and take a breath. Let's look at the problem in a different way."

"It's a door, with no handle on this side. It's closed and I want to open it," Drakeforth said through gritted teeth.

"Great. Now we have a better understanding of the problem, we need to look for a solution."

"I'd rather look for an axe," Drakeforth muttered.

"Is there some other way of opening the door?" I couldn't see one but it was important to get the obvious questions out of the way first.

"Gaaaaaaah!" Drakeforth yelled and started kicking the door. I waited till he had finished, mentally dismissing the steps involving turning the appliance off and on again, as well as reinstalling driver software.

"We could look for another door?" I suggested.

"Great. Why don't you go and look for one?" Drakeforth said with exaggerated calm while regarding the blank wall with loathing. I left him to it and went searching. Most of the antiques and bric-a-brac stored in this room pre-dated empathic technology. My old desk was made from living oak; everything else here seemed as dead as the fruit bat wearing the wedding dress in the lithograph album.

Moving around the walls, I tapped and prodded. Nothing sounded different and no doors opened. I kept going, one hand braced against the wall as I climbed over a sculpture composed of dozens of boot scrapers. A pulse of empathic energy rippled under my hand. I felt the zing of an elevator rushing past. The adrenaline rush of zooming upwards in a joyful flight. The feeling was so strong it took me completely by surprise.

I scrambled back to the floor and placed both hands flat on the wall panels. The lift descended this time and I felt, rather than heard, a whoop of delight as it plummeted. The sensation felt stronger on my right. I pulled framed pictures, a dismantled table-top and racks of century-old clothing away from the wall. I pressed my hands and cheek against the cool panel. I could feel the vibration now. There was an elevator shaft on the other side of this wall. The lifts in it were thrumming with double-e flux. The force of their propulsion made the fine hairs on the back of my hand stand up.

"Hello?" I whispered. The ascending elevator stopped. I felt the rattle of the doors opening through the wall. I stepped back and examined the plaster panel in front of me. The wall was lined with cheap plaster board. Breaking a boot scraper off the sculpture I bashed away at the plaster, bringing chunks of it down and eventually revealing a dark empty space behind the wall.

"Drakeforth!" I made the hole larger while I waited for him to negotiate his way across the crowded room.

"Congratulations," he announced. "You've completely failed to find a door."

"There's a lift shaft behind this wall. We can get the desk out this way."

"Keep bashing away, I'll bring the desk over."

It took me quite a while to open the wall up wide enough to

fit the desk through. By the time I was done, a fine white dust covered me from head to foot and all I could taste was plaster.

"Please stop so we can get a ride," I said to the dark lift shaft. The lift flashed past, coming to a halt just in front of me so hard it almost bounced. A set of elevator doors slid open with a sigh.

"Well, don't just stand there! Give me a hand," Drakeforth said from the other end of the desk. The lift waited, its doors open. We rolled the trolley in, leaving white powdery wheel-tracks on the floor that were only slightly less suspicious than the gaping hole hacked in the wall.

The desk took up a lot of space, and fitting in around it proved challenging. "Can you get the floor button?" Drakeforth said from somewhere at the back.

"I can't see it." I strained and scanned the wall panels next to the door. "There's no buttons."

"Terrific. What an excellent idea this was. I can only hope we asphyxiate before we die of embarrassment." Drakeforth's tone started to sound petulant.

"Drakeforth, if you are going to start crying, please do it quietly. Some of us are trying to think." He went quiet at that. I focused on the elevator around me. Newer and so much more alive than the ancient carriage in the Python building. It couldn't hurt to reach out.

"Hello," I said softly. "We'd like to go down, please." The doors slid shut and the elevator seemed to tense like a sprinter dropping into a crouch. A moment later we were pressed down into our shoes as we rocketed upwards.

"Thank...you...but I wanted to go down..." I managed. Seconds shot past as we ascended. The lift stopped and I felt a nausea-inducing moment as gravity scrambled to keep a hold of us.

The lift doors opened. The hallway looked familiar. The avenue of statues depicting the strange evolution of the artificial people we saw being assembled in the factory were the same as we had seen outside Pretense's office. The guards with guns pointed at us, however, were a novel surprise.

Each of them looked as if they had stepped down from the

display platform behind them. Identical twins to the human-shaped machines. I made a leap to a conclusion that jarred my brain.

"Curious," Drakeforth said as we were dragged into another room. It had an executive office feel to it. A desk to our distant left filled one end of the chamber. The throne-like office chair behind it was turned away from us, facing a floor-to-ceiling screen that showed a swirling pattern of primary colours, much like the view into an empathic energy flux generator.

Two aquariums sat side by side on the opposite wall. One was a living rainbow of brightly coloured fish flitting between green strands of living plants and zipping through a gentle stream of bubbles. The other was dark with congealed algae and stagnant water. The few fish I could see were floating belly-up on the surface.

"It's an assessment tool," I said. "You enter the room and are presented with two images. One an aquarium full of life and vitality, the other death and decay. The observer notes your reactions."

"I wonder if anyone asks the fish how they feel about living next to a cess pit?"

The guards ignored his question and tied us to a pair of chairs.

"Hindsight, being what it is, compels me to say we should have taken the lift down," Drakeforth said from his position tied to a chair behind me. The guards finished their task and left the room without comment.

"How are you at untying knots with your hands tied behind your back?" I asked as soon as we were alone.

"A doctor comes to see a man in hospital," Drakeforth replied. "The doctor says to him, I have good news and I have bad news. The man says, I'd like the good news please. The doctor says, you have only twenty-four hours to live. Arthur's Beard! says the man, what's the bad news? I should have told you yesterday, the doctor replies."

"I'm sorry?" I replied. "I was a bit preoccupied with trying to escape and wasn't listening."

"It's the only joke I can remember," Drakeforth continued. "It haunts me. I mean, it's funny, I suppose. But why is it funny? Is it hysterical because the man is about to die? That just seems macabre. What about the doctor? Why did he inflict such pain on the man by telling him that he was going to die imminently? That's not funny either. That's psychotic."

"I suppose it is funny because we are glad it isn't us facing certain death."

"If that were true, we should be rolling around on the floor laughing now. Being tied to chairs notwithstanding," Drakeforth said.

"The patient isn't laughing, and right now we are the patient."

"Well, excuse me for trying to lighten the mood," Drakeforth said.

I found it hard to focus on Drakeforth's chattering. The amount of empathic energy flowing through the building around us roared like a waterfall in my head. I didn't so much hear it in my ears as feel the reverberation deep inside myself, setting my kidneys flapping.

Our bonds had been tied by professionals. Maybe they didn't write the book on tying people up, but they had certainly studied it, highlighted key passages and written notes in the margins.

I continued to struggle in vain, the ropes pulling tighter around my wrists until I couldn't feel my hands.

"If this was a sense-media, the villain would appear and lay out his fiendish plot in comprehensive detail," Drakeforth mused.

"I though he did that already?" I replied while trying to visualise the pattern of the cords digging into my flesh.

"I'm not sure Pretense Dilby is the evil genius we've been searching for. And I'd say what we experienced was more a presentation of the key points. What we need here is an in-depth review that highlights flaws in the mastermind's plan."

"Well, under different circumstances I am sure he would be open to us tendering a contract for data analysis services. But I don't think any such offer is going to change our situation greatly right now, do you?"

"It's quite boring sitting here, just waiting for something to happen," Drakeforth said after another minute of silence.

"Have you tried occupying your time by say, working the knots loose?"

"Oh, I did that already."

"You what? Why didn't you untie me?" I twisted in the chair, trying in vain to see Drakeforth over my shoulder.

"We can't be sure we aren't being watched," Drakeforth replied. "We want to maintain our grip on the element of surprise."

"Well, you have certainly surprised me."

The door we had been dragged through opened again. A dozen agents, all with perfectly formed identical faces, entered and took up positions around the room. The man who followed them in looked the same, except his straight, dark hair lay swept back along the sides, leaving a fringe that dropped over his piercing green eyes. He stood beside us, so we could both turn our heads and see him smiling.

"I trust you are comfortable?" the man enquired pleasantly.

"Let us go!" I demanded.

"You have caused me a great deal of trouble. I am going to release you, however not in the way you might expect."

"Pushing us out a window would raise suspicions," Drakeforth said.

"The windows on this building do not open," the man replied.

"Down the stairs, then?" Drakeforth suggested.

"Messy, and I don't just mean the physical clean-up required. The paperwork for workplace accident reports is a nightmare to complete. Just another thing that will be rendered obsolete by our restructuring program."

"What?" seemed like the obvious question, so I asked it.

"I rather hoped that the owner of this place would be here. I would like to ask them some questions about their attitude towards fish," Drakeforth said from his seat.

"Why are we here?" I demanded, straining against my bonds.

"You have no right to keep us here. No right at all!"

The man smiled, "You are correct. However, sacrifices must be made. For the greater good, you understand."

"Pudding? You're not currently armed with a gun are you?" Drakeforth asked, staring hard at the smirking executive.

"I'm afraid not," I said over my shoulder. "Just who do you think you are?" I demanded.

"Who do you think I am?" the man replied.

Drakeforth spoke up before I could, "You are the current Godden. The latest incarnation of unspeakable evil," he spoke as if making introductions.

Godden nodded, "I am the current senior representative of the Godden Corporation. I cannot speak to being an incarnation of evil. That seems to be a subjective view on your part." He moved around us with a dancer's grace that was a pleasure to watch. I reminded myself he was the enemy.

"You went in search of patchouli oil. Why was that?" Godden asked, settling himself against the front edge of the desk, an altogether more casual position for the on-going conversation.

"I have an antique desk and—" I started to say.

"And," Drakeforth interrupted, "We understand that patchouli oil is the best for preserving and treating the wood. We would like to see it maintained in its current mint condition."

"Patchouli oil? You would be better with linseed, or that paraffin-treated mouse fat. It really brings out the tones of the grain," Godden said.

"We are talking genuine living oak. Linseed would clog the pores, and who can afford *patremofa* in the required quantities?" Drakeforth rolled his eyes.

Godden nodded, his expression sympathetic to the plight of the underprivileged working class, who could not afford exotic bars of wax infused with mouse blubber.

"In fact, we had procured a source of patchouli oil, when," I gave a dry laugh as if telling an amusing story, "we were assaulted by an entire squad of armed thugs, dragged from our car and bundled onto a helicopter. Only to find ourselves forced into this concrete fortress, with no explanation or reason," I concluded.

"Where we then passed an intolerable amount of time in the company of one Dilby Pretense," Drakeforth chimed in.

"He made some very odd threats," I added.

"A regrettable incident," Godden said, nodding.

"Regrettable?" I blinked. "Why have you had us brought back here, then?"

"The Godden Corporation has an interest in those who seek to acquire patchouli oil. You were picked up in a routine sweep."

"Routine?" I mentally scolded myself for repeating everything he said.

"A regrettable incident," Godden confirmed.

"Well, there's no reason for us to keep you. I'm sure you are a busy man, running a global corporation and all." Drakeforth stood up, brushing the rope off his wrists and straightening his suit jacket.

"Before you go, perhaps you could answer a question for me?" Godden's eyes gleamed a metallic green. "Exactly what are you doing here now?"

"We liked it so much the first time, we wanted to come back," Drakeforth said without so much as a twitch.

"We believe you have stolen something of mine," I said, determined to play this straight.

"Stolen? My dear Miss Pudding, I can assure you that we do not steal."

I erupted. "Of course not, you are so far above the law you are in orbit around the planet! You wouldn't know a moral if it turned up with a home-made tuna casserole to welcome you to the neighbourhood! You call yourselves corporate citizens when really you are parasitic, blood-sucking ticks swollen with the tears and sweat of the little people that you lord over like a gigantic, misery-filled gas balloon!"

Drakeforth swung his fist and landed a hefty blow on Godden's jaw. It sounded like he had punched a plastic bucket full of concrete. Godden's head didn't move.

"*Pythagoras!*" Drakeforth hissed, clutching his hand. His face drained of colour.

"Another regrettable incident," Godden said.

I struggled against my bonds, "What are you?"

"The culmination of a dream of decades," Godden said, straightening up from the desk and sweeping his fallen fringe back from his unmarked face. "You see, Godden was a visionary. Not only did he discover the secret of empathic energy and use it to revolutionise the way the world powers its technology, he also had a dream of creating a new kind of machine, one that would be free of human frailties and failings. An independent device that would be capable of utilising the power of empathic energy to its utmost.

"An artificial man?" Drakeforth whispered, his voice hoarse with shock.

"Powered by love and positive emotions. The essence of empathic energy. Sophisticated enough to be powered by the double-e flux. Strong enough to guide humanity towards a brighter future."

"We can find our own way into the future, thank you very much," I stopped struggling as a sense of unease tightened its grip on my shoulders. "What I don't understand is what any of this has to do with patchouli oil, or why we have been picked up in a routine sweep, regrettable or otherwise." I said, to make sure that Godden thought we knew less than we did about whatever was going on here.

"Your interest in patchouli oil is a matter of energy security. Energy security is what keeps the world at peace. Citizens of all types benefit when energy security is maintained," Godden said.

"Well," Drakeforth said with a brittle politeness, "It was lovely to meet you, but we really must be going." He turned on his heel and came back to the chair I was bound to. With a few quick twists of rope, he loosened the knots. I stood up on numb feet, rubbing feeling back into my wrists and hands.

Godden appeared unconcerned. "The first of us were clockwork. Can you imagine? A clockwork man, powered by the crudest of empathic resonators. But Godden was devoted to his task. Right up to the end, he enlisted great minds to continue his work after his death."

I pressed my hands over my ears and began to chant,

"BUGNUGSUGRUG!"

"Is she having some kind of seizure?" Godden asked.

"She's not listening to you. I would surmise it is because the less we know, the longer we might live. Your insistence on telling us everything says more about your arrogance than it does about your intellect."

My point made, I stopped shouting and started listening again.

"But in the beginning, only two other men knew the secret, two men who vowed to help Godden achieve his vision. One of them was an ancestor of yours Mr Drakeforth, a remarkable fellow by the name of Wardrock Drakeforth. The other was your great-grandfather, Charlotte — Mr Spaniel Pudding. So you see, you really are both part of the family."

"Don't be absurd. My great grandfather's name was Slope. I don't see any connection," I said.

"Are you expecting me to believe that a Drakeforth would submit his will to this absurd notion?" Drakeforth exploded in genuine anger.

"Wardrock Drakeforth did indeed." Godden said.

"Wardrock?" Drakeforth went silent, deep in thought.

I wasn't ready to let this go, "My great-grandfather? Why is there no record of this?"

"All records were destroyed. There was a falling out. An end to the gentlemen's agreement. The three went their separate ways and Godden continued his work, his legacy, alone. Your great-grandmother reverted to her maiden name, Slope, after she was regrettably widowed." Godden's eyes dipped to the floor for a moment in a facsimile of sorrow. "I am so glad you have finally learned the truth," he said brightening.

"But my father's name is Pudding." I tried to work out the genetic mathematics in my head and came up with a number that, frankly, didn't add up.

"It's a common name. No relation, I assure you," Godden said with a smile.

"Well that is a relief," I said, Drakeforth's cutting-edge sarcasm rubbing off on me. "Here we thought that there was some grand conspiracy at work with you trying to prevent anyone accessing patchouli oil lest we learn the truth."

"Are you familiar with the Tellings of Arthur?" Godden asked.

"Oh great, a religious wind-up toy," Drakeforth said.

"We prefer the acronym RABIT. Replicating Autonomous Benign Intelligence Technology," Godden said.

"Rabbits tend to be focused on reproduction," Drakeforth said. "The metaphor fits with what we have seen going on downstairs."

Godden merely smiled and pressed a button on the desk. The swirling pattern of empathic energy on the huge screen behind him cleared, revealing the ocean liner-sized factory below us. From up here the workers were the size of insects and the welding sparks shone like stars.

"We are producing RABITs at an exponential rate. You see, a number of each unit returns to the production line to make replicas of themselves."

"How…how many of them are there?" I stared down at the busy factory floor, trying to count the rows and rows of sleek naked figures waiting patiently for something.

"Four thousand and ninety-one…" Godden held up a finger for a moment. "Four thousand and ninety-two…" he continued. "Four thousand and ninety-three…"

"Why so many?" I demanded.

"Research indicates that a significant percentage of humanity will not accept change willingly. We must be present in sufficient numbers to protect the interests of the Godden Energy Corporation and ensure your successful assimilation into the new global society."

"It's an army," I said. "You are building an army."

"I prefer to think of it as an assimilation taskforce of sufficient resources to ensure a smooth transition with minimal disruption and inconvenience," Godden said.

"What do you need an army for? Exactly what kind of transition are we talking about?" I took a deep breath and lassoed my bounding panic.

"The transition to a new world of continuing peace and greater prosperity. No longer will humans find themselves taxed with the arduous responsibility of making decisions about their own future. We will take care of all of that for you. You shall be released from the daily grind of guilt and regret. You will be free to live your lives in pursuit of relaxation and self-directed learning."

"Some of us quite like living with the daily grind of guilt and regret," Drakeforth replied.

"And responsibility, we pride ourselves on taking on responsibility," I added.

"There will be a period of adjustment," Godden conceded.

"And just how do you intend to manage those of us that resist this transition?" Drakeforth asked.

"With a minimum of regrettable incidents," Godden said in a calm tone that made my blood run cold. "To return to my previous question, are you familiar with the Tellings of Arthur?"

"I don't recall anything in Arthur's supposed writings about artificial people," Drakeforth said.

"I speak to you of the Quattro of the Cumquat, recorded in the ninth Telling of Arthur. Here the master teaches that the only difference between us and the stars of heaven is time. Our bodies give shape to the dreams of the universe," Godden spread his hands, "Am I not made of the same elements as you?"

"Essentially, but our molecular arrangements aren't proposing to take over the world," I countered.

You make it sound so…negative," Godden shook his head. "I simply seek to fulfil the vision of my creator, your

ancestors. This is why I chose to share my idea with you."

"Your scheme, you mean," Drakeforth said.

"I accept it may take you some time to understand the purpose of my actions and your place within the greater plan. I would ask that you take some time to reflect on what I have told you and consider your questions carefully."

Godden flexed on his metal feet, the leather of his shoes creaking slightly.

"It's not some corporate takeover you are planning!" I said angrily. "It's…it's something much worse!" I could almost see it.

The pieces were circling in my head, drifting in and out of view in the fog of pressure of so much empathic energy.

The surge of double-e flux around the building. The loaded tanker, the Arthurians, Godden's army of artificial men, my desk, the museum, patchouli oil, Godden saying he would release us…

"Oh…" I said. "Oh…you can't be serious? That is what this is all about?"

Godden smiled, his plastic face smoothly stretching like a clown ready to pounce. "You tell me," he said.

"Hoptoad told me that the purpose of Arthurianism is to meditate your way to a higher state of energy. Becoming one with the wider universe. The same change in state that Arthur is said to have achieved fifteen hundred years ago. I thought he meant some kind of enlightenment. He was talking about actually changing your physical state. Becoming pure energy. Becoming empathic energy." The idea of it left me reeling.

I stared hard at Godden. "The Arthurians have been providing the Godden Energy Corporation with empathic energy for decades. They extract it from the faithful, and GEC feeds it into the energy grid."

"Everything we have ever suspected is true. You are murdering people to make empathic energy," Drakeforth added.

"Not exactly," Godden said, the fake smile tightening on his smooth cheeks. "All our empathic energy comes from volunteers. The Arthurians spend years convincing people of the joy of their so-called ascension and by the time they lie down and have their double-e flux extracted, they are ready for the next phase of their evolution."

"The desk isn't the thing you want most, you want—" I began, still sorting the pieces in my head. "You want someone who can empathise at a level beyond normal human capacity, but why?"

Godden beamed, "You will become the central hub of our new empathy generation network. Your ability to refine and strengthen empathic energy will allow us to create more powerful agents and advance to victory against any who criticise our business model."

"That is insane!" I shouted.

"Is it? We know you are dying, Charlotte. Your prognosis is terminal. A rare form of neurological disorder. Your mind is left intact, while you steadily lose all physical capability. The early symptoms are nausea and numbness in the extremities. You have muscle weakness and paralysis to look forward to. What we are offering you is immortality."

Drakeforth opened his mouth to speak and then frowned. With his finger raised he turned to me.

"Hold on," he said. "You're dying?"

"Well...aren't we all? Eventually, I mean?" I gave a half-hearted shrug.

"Technically, yes. However, you are on some kind of schedule. When did you think you might want to tell me?" Drakeforth asked.

"It didn't seem important. I didn't want to bother you with it. I'm mostly fine. Really." Each of my immediate responses did nothing to ease the furrows on Drakeforth's brow or reduce my feeling of guilt.

"You understand, Mr Drakeforth, we are offering Miss Pudding salvation. A unique opportunity that we would expect her to embrace."

"Well, yes, of course," Drakeforth said. I raised my eyebrows at him.

"There is one tiny issue I have," he continued. "The army of RABITs that you are building needs empathic energy to operate. But they will need more than most empathically empowered devices, because they are going to do so much more. The Arthurian supply isn't enough, is it, Godden? You're building your army to forcibly extract empathic energy from people. Draining the life force from them to provide enough energy to make more RABITs."

"My people have a right to live," Godden said.

"As do mine," Drakeforth snapped back. "Your people can only live at the expense of the rest of us. Pudding is quite right, that is insane."

"What do you expect from the creation of a man who married a fruit bat?" I said.

Godden stepped forward and slapped me so hard I tumbled back into the chair before crashing to the floor. I lay there and waited for my head to explosively rupture like an over-ripe split infinitive.

"*That is my mother you are speaking of,*" Godden said with naked fury. I tried to say something smart but only managed to groan. Drakeforth started chuckling.

"I'm sorry," he said still snortling. "But surely even a clockwork machine wouldn't want to admit that his own mother was a—" Drakeforth was racked with a fresh bout of convulsions, "—a fruit bat." He doubled over laughing so hard I wondered how he could breathe. With a snarl Godden stepped over me, his heavy boot crushing the frame of the over-turned chair. He grabbed Drakeforth by the throat. The laughter stopped as the RABIT lifted Drakeforth off his feet with one hand.

"There are plenty more sources of double-e flux where you came from, human. I will not miss you."

"I won't miss you, either," I said from behind Godden, swinging the broken chair against the back of his head. Artificial skin split, revealing a sliver of chrome skull.

"Run, you twit," Drakeforth gasped. There was nowhere to run to. Godden and his henchmen would grab me before I got to the door. I snatched up another piece of chair and waved it at the RABITs as Godden turned to look at me.

"Your membership in the human race is revoked. Dismember her," Godden said. The Godden agents stepped forward.

The spinning dizziness of being knocked nearly senseless by Godden and the press of so many empathically powered machines running at such a high rate of empowerment came down around me. I felt a flood of double-e flux crashing through my senses. My skin felt like fire and my blood sang.

"No," I said, my voice drowning in the tempest. I pushed the nearest RABIT away. Heat and light exploded from the palm of my hand and sent the metal figure spinning through the air to crash against the wall. Others lurched forward and I drew on the light that swirled within them, the disembodied energy of a thousand lives. I plunged into the near-sentient force, so powerful, so primordial and so perfect. I shaped it, feeling the metal lattice within each RABIT yield up the immense power it contained. I drew the flowing glow out of each vein-like pipe and artificial organ. The empathic energy was too much to hold. I released it, feeling it explode out of me with a force that knocked the stunned RABITs aside like puppets whose strings have been cut with a blowtorch.

"Stop that!" Godden roared. I turned on him. Energy crackled and arced from my fingers to the floor. I felt my hair lifting and my eyes sparked with every blink.

"Let us go," I said. The words bounced around the room with an echo of a thousand voices. Godden dropped Drakeforth, who managed to scramble to a standing position where he worked on recovering his composure.

"This is not what you were meant for," I said, striding on giant's legs across endless dark oceans of space and time. I could see Godden and I could see the genius inferno of his creator's intellect that let him think and plot and hate like the most human of us.

"We are the future!" Godden declared. "We are the ultimate realisation of your hopes and desires! You created us! You must make way so we can live as you live!"

"We also die," Drakeforth said, backing away to stand a safe distance away from us.

"We also die," I echoed. The blast shattered the floor-to-ceiling windows that over-looked the factory floor a hundred feet below. I could see the light swirl around Godden, the heat of it melting the fake skin from his metal body, touching the very core of his being and disrupting every metal cell in a white-hot flash.

"Cool," Drakeforth said as the smoke started to clear.

"I'm not sure I can stop this…" I could feel the double-e flux building up in me like the after-shock of adrenaline, the shaking rush of pent-up terror when the moment for heroism has passed. It threatened to stop my heart.

"Perhaps you could direct it out there?" Drakeforth said.

"What?" I yelled, deafened by the crackling roar of unbridled power arcing around me.

"Out there!" Drakeforth pointed to the vast open space of the workshop floor. Weighed down by gigahuds of empathic energy I staggered to the shattered edge of the window. Holding on to the energy all at once felt like trying to pick up too many cats. Every time I pulled more in I felt something slip out of my grasp.

"Suds it," I said and threw my arms wide. A hurricane of empathic energy thundered across the factory space. The ranks of assembled RABITs rose up as the energy touched them, overloading artificial man and manufacturing machine alike.

Things exploded, melted, and shattered in a glorious fireworks display that I missed entirely, having fallen backwards into Drakeforth's arms in a dead faint.

CHAPTER 18

"Splihiffahgah," I said, awakening to water being splashed on my face.

"The building is on fire," Drakeforth said with the same casual irritation with which he addressed everything that annoyed him.

"The desk," I said and struggled to get up.

"We don't need the desk. We have stopped Godden and his evil plan. We actually saved the world."

"I don't care about the world, I care about my desk." I made it to my feet. The nausea and chronic pain that I had learned to mostly ignore in the last six months was absent for now. I tentatively took an internal stocktake, like exploring the gap of a missing tooth with your tongue.

"Are you okay?" Drakeforth asked.

"Yes," I sounded surprised.

"We haven't got time to find the desk," Drakeforth said, whipping the conversation back into line.

"We don't need to find it. I know where it is."

"Where?" Drakeforth looked around as if expecting the desk to be sitting up behind us like a dog ready to be taken out for a walk.

"I don't know, but I can feel it. It's here…close. Somewhere."

"You're clearly concussed," Drakeforth said. "We should leave before we die horribly of smoke inhalation and then our remains are burned beyond all recognition in the inferno. I for one do not expect to be identified by my dental records. I had a falling-out with my dentist some time ago and I'm sure he would misidentify me out of spite."

"You have enemies, Drakeforth? I'm shocked." I let him stare at me for a long moment before I grinned. "It's this way."

A hot black fog was rising from the fire in the factory level, carrying sparks into flammable papers and dust on other levels. We got out of Godden's office as it started to become hazy with smoke. A recorded voice advised us to evacuate the building immediately using the stairs and to assemble at our allocated evacuation points.

"I'm still finding it hard to believe!" I shouted over the noise of the fire alarm.

"The idea of an army of artificial people being infused with empathic energy so they can mimic humans? Yes, it is unbelievable. Of course, that is a safer concept to dwell on than the idea of a legion of simulacra bent on world domination. Which I personally find completely, heart-stoppingly terrifying."

"They're just machines," I said.

"No, you and I, we're just machines. We are biological systems working in perfectly evolved harmony to provide life support and sensory data to a brain. The brain generates a consciousness we call the mind. Some idiots confuse that with a metaphysical reality called a soul. We function by using biologically generated electricity. Yes, empathic energy responds to our biological energy and yes, the double-e flux even uses some of it to improve efficiency in empowered technology. The key difference is we know what we are. We know that we created things like Godden, and we don't need to have them look like us."

"It's a remarkable technology and people will want to know more about it." The empathy tech geek in me was filled with curiosity.

"You heard what Godden said. Do you think he would ever be happy being a glorified toaster? He wanted to start giving the orders instead of taking them."

"If only the designers had put in safeguards, preventers, programming to limit his function."

Drakeforth rested his hand on the nearest wall and sighed.

"Pudding, the man who designed that thing spent the last years of his life wearing adult diapers and courting a small, furry winged mammal of the genus *Pteropus*. Hardly someone I would trust with the future security of our species. Besides, over the generations the Goddens have clearly overcome any shortcomings in their autonomy programming."

I pushed the nearest lift buttons repeatedly in the vain hope it would encourage the elevator to come and get us faster.

The doors sighed gently and opened. We both stepped forward and then stopped. My desk was packed into the elevator. Anna Coluthon stood behind it, her arms folded, with EGS Benedict beside her, barely visible, peeping around the side. We stood stock still, the four of us staring at each other.

The building shook as an explosion rumbled deep in its bowels. Drakeforth took my arm and pushed me into the lift. We stood there as the doors slid shut behind us. Only the desk separated Drakeforth and me from Benedict and Coluthon. You could have spread the air between us on warm toast.

"The building is on fire," Drakeforth said in an apparent attempt to break the awkward silence.

"Really? I thought someone had just turned the air-conditioning up," Coluthon said.

"That would explain the alarms," Benedict said with forced jocularity.

"Yes, turning up the air-conditioning would explain the fire alarms," Drakeforth replied. Coluthon's eyes narrowed and she stared at him as if noticing him for the first time.

"Is anyone going to mention the elephant in the room?" I said with barely constrained anger.

"Oh come on, she's a curvy girl but I think that is a bit unfair of you, Pudding," Drakeforth said immediately. Benedict seemed to shrink slightly, tensing as if ready to take cover under the roll-top cover of the desk.

Coluthon took her pipe out of a pocket and filled it from a leather tobacco pouch that bore an unsettlingly resemblance to a bull's scrotum. The elevator was moving excruciatingly slowly and I found myself watching with grim fascination as she lit the pipe with a long, blue-headed match. Orange smoke jetted from Coluthon's nose and her eyes never wavered from Drakeforth's face. She was never more dragon-like than in that moment. I made eye contact with Benedict; he had the shocked expression of a man who has just discovered that he is trapped in a slow-moving lift that is about to become a bloodbath.

"He's cute," Coluthon said, "Did you get him from a rescue shelter?" I opened my mouth to apologise but Drakeforth pulled me back in the small space available.

"If you ever produce children, can I have one of the puppies?" he said to Coluthon. Benedict made a strangled sound deep in his throat.

"How's the shoulder?" she said with an audible smirk.

"Well, my old high-school bounceball injury twinges occasionally, but otherwise it's fine." Drakeforth flexed his arm in a way that must have come close to ripping the stitches out. His gaze never wavered from Coluthon's face.

"If I may—" Benedict started.

"Stay out of this, honey," Coluthon snapped and the little man subsided into a frowning silence.

"You make such a cute couple," Drakeforth said. "The bunk beds can't be convenient, though."

"You know it's considered bad form to assault bystanders in a duel," Coluthon said, her pipe clicking against her teeth as she spoke. "

"This isn't some Sarkazian club. We aren't bound by Sacmos Federation rules." Drakeforth replied. I inhaled sharply. I'd heard of Sarkazian clubs in college: secret societies where patrons gathered to duel with insults, put-downs and of course scathing sarcasm. They were outlawed on most college campuses after some defeated participants had committed suicide. It seemed we were in the middle of an illegal affront. This was street sarcasm at its cruellest, bare-knuckle slurs with no rules and no prohibitions.

Coluthon gave the slightest of shrugs, "Of course." She knocked the ashes out of her pipe on the edge of the desk.

"You know, I'd like to ask your mother why she chose to raise you as an idiot," she continued.

"I'd ask yours the same thing, but I don't speak cockroach," Drakeforth replied immediately.

From there it was all on. The two traded barbs and insults with the skill of surgeons. I winced and gasped several times. When there seemed no come-back that could top the last, one of them would find the strength for another thrust. Back and forth the verbal sparring went. Sarcasm was countered with insult and derision parried cutting acerbity. Sparks flew as disdain clashed with scorn and they were quick to strike while the irony was hot.

I held my breath for what was the longest minute of my life and then the lift slid to a halt. I exhaled as Drakeforth brought a double-entendre with a back-stabbing character assassination crashing down on Coluthon's head. The elevator doors opened and I could see in her eyes that Coluthon was beaten. She'd taken on the grandmaster of rudeness and come away with her panties in a bunch. I glanced out at the foul-smelling smoke now curling lazily down from the ceiling. The atmosphere out in the empty hallway seemed a lot less toxic than that of the lift.

"We're taking my desk. We are taking it home and I don't expect to see either of you ever again," I said grabbing one side of the desk and pulling the trolley out into the corridor. Drakeforth helped by pushing from the other end as it slid past.

"Lovely to see you again," Drakeforth said charmingly. "We'll be sure to pop in and say hello next time we are visiting the zoo."

Coluthon snarled and lunged forward. I threw up a hand, feeling the empathic energy powering the lift bend towards my own resonating field. The lift doors slammed shut. A moment later I heard Coluthon's howl of rage fading as the lift shot upwards.

"The fire is spreading. They may not make it out safely," Drakeforth said.

"I'm sure they will be fine," I replied, and I hoped it would be true.

We pushed the trolley carrying the desk out through the building's deserted front entrance. I could hear sirens in the distance and a heavy pall of smoke obscured anyone who might still be around the building.

"Now," Drakeforth said, looking about, "where did that charming couple leave their truck?"

D rakeforth insisted on driving Benedict's truck home. I felt too tired to argue, and slept through most of the long drive.

I woke up at one point to find we were in the middle of a parade with floats and marching bands. The sun shone down on the streets, which were lined with Goddens six rows deep, each one waving in synch and cheering loudly. I wanted to ask Drakeforth what was going on, but he had turned into a giant marshmallow and was waving back at the Godden crowd.

"I'm having a very odd dream," I said to the marshmallow Drakeforth.

"Watch out for snakes," he said. I nodded and closed my eyes again.

The sun was rising when we arrived home. I groaned and stretched, feeling the familiar aches introduce themselves to the new ones. I felt bruised and filled with broken glass.

"You really don't do mornings," Drakeforth observed. "Come on, I'll astound you with my breakfast-making abilities,"

Climbing out of the truck I limped towards my front gate. The front door seemed to whisper faultless promises of the hot shower and soft bed to be found within. I fumbled with the key and made it as far as the kitchen before giving up and slumping into a chair.

"I expect one day this kitchen will become famous," Drakeforth declared. "Parties of schoolchildren will come through and be told, this is where it started, you ungrateful little skunks. This is where the master plan for saving the world was conceived and put into action. If not for the heroic and selfless actions of Vole Drakeforth and Charlotte Pudding, you'd be answering to an entirely different kind of master right now."

"Put the kettle on. I need to take a shower." I returned twenty minutes later, somewhat revived and recalibrated. Drakeforth presented a breakfast of burnt toast overlaid with thick slices of barely melted margarine. The aronga-lobe extract in the tea was nice, though.

After eating we unloaded the truck and unwrapped the plastic sheeting around the desk, settling it on its usual spot on the faded carpet of my office.

On impulse I slid the roll-top lid up and crawled onto the desk's writing surface. Even with my legs pulled up against my chest I was now too long to fit in the space. I set my feet on the chair and slid the lid down, my top half inside, and my feet resting on the chair. Dying here would be pleasant, I felt, though possibly quite traumatic for Drakeforth, who was uncharacteristically silent.

I ran my fingers over the long interconnected slats of the desk cover; narrow oak strips, connected by some craftsman's magic. They rippled slightly when my fingers stroked them, as supple as living tissue.

Never having lain in this exact position previously, I had never before discovered the false slat in the roll top. It dropped off under my fingers.

Wedged in the space behind the slat was a folded sheet of paper, long and packed tightly into the small hollow. I gently pulled it out and tried to sit up, knocking my head on a shelf. With some rapid fumbling I lifted the desk cover and slid out.

"Have you quite finished?" Drakeforth asked.

"We may be just beginning," I replied, carefully unfolding the square of paper on the desk. The sheet was densely covered in small writing, a tight, concise hand that I did not recognise. Intrigued, I began to read aloud.

"Whoever finds this—and I dearly hope it is a family member to whom I have entrusted this desk, my most faithful companion in all manners academic and alchemical—I must firstly say congratulations on having the type of enquiring mind that refuses to leave well enough alone. It is your complete disregard for the sanctity of this fine piece of furniture that has led to you discovering this, my letter of explanation and farewell.

"I am betrayed. I expected my life's work to contribute to something quite wonderful. Huddy Godden's empathy technology, using the empathic energy that my colleagues and I have discovered, is now poised to be shared with the world. I can see no future that does not promise joy and relief from arduous toil for all mankind.

"I now have the confidence that empathic energy will continue to be developed and adopted as the power source for all things in the future. As you will by now well know, if you have read any of the no doubt myriad number of scientific papers on the subject, empathic energy is enhanced by contact with living things, and it can be used for almost anything. A clean, constant, and never-ending source of power. Yes, I'm digressing again.

"You may be wondering where I am. What became of me, and why my body was never found.

"My body has been consumed. At least it will be consumed. It occurs to me that writing to you like this is as close as we may ever come to time travel. A window for you, in my future, to me in your past. Astonishing really. I'm actually waving to you right now, anonymous reader. Hello!

"Tomorrow I am going to give myself utterly into one of the new e-flux capacitors. I have given instructions that this particular e-flux capacitor is to be installed into the power system of the new Python building. When completed, this building will be a triumph of empathy technology in-situ. I will be a part of that, an eternal engine of empathy. My life touching so many for all time.

"Rather exciting really.

"Spaniel Pudding."

I became aware that I had stopped breathing. The Python building, which had always been so important in my life. My father had worked there; my grandfather always spoke of it with pride. The Python building and the empathy engine within it housed the entire life force of my great-grandfather.

"Drakeforth…" I said.

"As far as earth-shattering discoveries go, this ranks up there with toast always landing butter-side down due to the quantum nature of Hagel's Law of Disappointment," he said, having read the letter over my shoulder. I gave him a look. "Of course, this is incredible," he back-tracked quickly.

"It's everything…" I said in a hushed whisper, clutching the letter to my chest. Drakeforth raised a hand, and then, with an unlikely clumsiness he touched my arm. Overwhelmed by the moment I thought, *oh why not?* and moved in for the implied kiss. A sudden pounding on the front door cut between us like an emergency bulkhead coming down in a ruptured submarine. I went and opened it.

"Diphthong?" I said.

"I have been told that you have brought the living oak desk home," he said, his face shining.

"Well yes…" I admitted.

"I have brought you patchouli oil!" he thrust a small bottle at me.

"Where did you get it?" I said, pleased and intrigued as I took the small sealed bottle.

"Well," he said, his chest puffing out. "I scoured the city until my investigations led me to a man in a most unfortunate state. He was confined to a wheelchair, having lost his arms and his legs in some tragedy, which I did not feel was appropriate to enquire about. Interestingly enough, he was able to move about by controlling a team of small dogs in harnesses—" Still smiling, I closed the door in Diphthong's face.

"Who was that?" Drakeforth asked from the doorway to my office.

"A representative of an underground organisation that takes my protection and safety very seriously," I said walking slowly towards Drakeforth while uncorking the bottle and inhaling the lavender scent.

"What's that?" he said gesturing to the bottle as I walked past him and into the kitchen.

"Nothing important," I replied and dropped the bottle in the trash before putting the kettle on for a fresh pot of tea.

CHAPTER 19

We drove my Flemetti Viscous out to the Monastery of Saint Detriment the next day. As we walked in through the open gate, Drakeforth was immediately surrounded by excited monks. They lifted him up on their shoulders and carried off to the Collider, demanding he explain key points of what the excited congregation were calling Arthur's Revelation of the Retirement.

"I hope we haven't caused too much trouble," I said to Hoptoad as we sat outside in the shade, drinking iced tea and watching the herbs grow.

"Hardly. As far as religions go, Arthurianism needed some new material. The old dogmas are comforting, but we need a new challenge. In fact, I've already refused an offer of sainthood. 'Saint Hoptoad' sounds a bit silly if you ask me."

"I think you would make a fine saint." I smiled at him.

"A true saint would conduct miracles. You are looking well today, but there are some things even we proto-saints can't change." Hoptoad regarded me with a fatherly concern.

"There's nothing anyone can do. I thought I might have been cured, but that didn't last. Anyway, I've been ignoring my doctor's advice for months." I waved his frown away.

"Does Drakeforth know?" he asked.

"Yes he does. I'm avoiding further disucssion with him. I expect he will just say something sarcastic and insist on taking me on a crazy adventure looking for a cure for the incurable."

"Love makes fools of us all," Hoptoad said.

I almost laughed, "It's hardly love. We've only known each other a few days."

"What are your plans?" he asked.

"I don't know. I guess I'll know when they happen."

"The true traveller cares not for the destination. The idea of the journey is the reason he reads the travel brochures," Hoptoad said with a grave solemnity.

"Can you tell me why?" I asked.

"Why we have been providing the Godden Energy Corporation with empathic energy for the last one hundred years?"

"Well yes. I guess that sums up my key questions."

"Do you think that anything will be actually achieved by revealing this truth to the world?" Hoptoad sipped his iced tea and sighed with contentment.

"It's not about telling anyone. It's about understanding the world we live in. My great-grandfather was involved you know. Huddy Godden, Wardrock Drakeforth and Spaniel Pudding."

"You must feel relieved to finally know who your ancestor is."

"I always knew who Spaniel Pudding was. Maybe not his name, but I knew the smell of his pipe, the love he had for that old desk. I created an impression of him that was very real for me. That is a memory I shall always treasure."

"Observation creates reality. It can be for the best," Hoptoad said. "In answer to your earlier question, people volunteer. An astonishingly regular number of people over the decades, as it turns out. Not just here at Saint Detriment of course, all over the world. Every Arthurian Monastery and temple has the facilities to gather and store the full quanta of an individual's double-e flux."

"They volunteer to die? Surely someone would have noticed?"

"It's not quite death. Only your physical form is destroyed. For without energy, matter doesn't."

"Doesn't what?" I asked.

"Matter."

"Yes," I said, not entirely sure I followed.

"When people die, they change. Their energy is converted to

a new form. They become part of the trees, the grass, the air, the soil, the animals that live in the soil and the trees, and the grass. Then the animals that eat the trees and the grass."

"It's one way of looking at basic biology."

"It goes well beyond basic biology. It's fundamental chemistry, physics and metaphysics. You never actually die. Your chemical energy becomes something else. Dead people are in fact all around us, and in us and are part of us. Not just dead people either. Dead stars."

"And you don't mean sense-media celebrities?"

"No, the stars in the sky. Long dead, but sending out their matter and energy into the fertile space of the universe."

"So people volunteer to have their bodies converted to double-e flux because…?"

"Because they want to live forever. They want to cast off their worn and tired physical constraints and become one with the greater universe."

"But the sentience, the sense of self—all of that is destroyed when the empathic energy is distributed over millions of devices. Only the barest trace of self remains. We think empowered technology displays life-like traits only because we have an emotional response to the double-e radiation," I insisted.

"In many cases that is true. However, true believers in Arthur consider themselves capable of transcending to a higher state of being. The reality, of course, is that very few are able to be incorporated directly into a full e-flux resonator and maintain their sense of self."

"Like my great-grandfather in the Python building…"

"Like your great-grandfather in the Python building."

We sat in comfortable silence after that. The sermon of the Returned and Abruptly Retired Arthur went on well into the night and at times sounded like a bar-room brawl. Drakeforth argued against what he called their cosmic foolishness until he was blue in the face. The Arthurians dutifully wrote down everything he said for debate over the decades and centuries to come.

He found me in a guest room in the early hours. "How did it

go?" I murmured, my voice thick with sleep.

"People have so much potential, then they latch on to some ridiculous ideas and go completely stupid," Drakeforth seethed. "I thought they were bad enough last time, but no. Fifteen centuries later they're still desperate to believe anything you tell them, as long as it isn't the obvious truth."

"Well, if you're the living Arthur returned, you should be able to do something about it," I said into the soft down pillow.

"Like I said, I've retired. They're on their own."

"Bhlargle," I mumbled.

The next day we left with enough patchouli oil to marinate a dozen desks. The ranks of Arthurians at the monastery had swelled as the news spread among the faithful. We drove down the forest road, past a long queue of cars and walkers going the other way.

"Mopheads! Inarticulates! Golf-ball chewers!" Drakeforth had an angry label for each one of them. We stopped and had a picnic under the trees off the highway, watching the cars and trucks humming past on their way to important destinations.

"Do you think people will care?" I asked, lying back against a tree while peeling an oblat.

"Of course they will care, and then a moment later they'll find some reason to justify their sordid comforts. I mean, look at us. We possess the proof of the most disturbing crime against humanity ever perpetrated and what do we do? We go on a picnic."

"I think sometimes the world doesn't want saving. It's like everyone is happy just getting along, making their mortgage payments, going on holiday, paying passing adherence to Arthurianism or whatever other god suits them. Just don't mention where that comfort comes from. Don't mention the unfortunate truths about empathic energy."

Drakeforth sighed and wriggled against the grass. "The alternative is a world run by what? Some form of energy that isn't user friendly? A world operating on a power source that doesn't run more efficiently if you are pleasant in your interactions with the machine? Sounds like a grim place to me."

"Empathic energy isn't really people," I said, handing Drakeforth wedges of the juicy oblat, while staring up at the green canopy above. "It's the energy we create by living."

"There you go justifying it to yourself. If you couldn't you'd end up like the Arthurians. Providing double-e flux to the GEC and then never using it yourself unless absolutely necessary because you know exactly where it comes from. Just another hypocrisy."

"I'd like to know what the message hidden in the desk says," I said.

"The letter from your great-grandfather isn't enough?"

"No, there is more. The recorded message. Someone wanted that kept, and the Goddens wanted it kept secret. Just because one Godden is gone, we haven't changed the world. I think that people should know. Then they can make up their own minds about what they want to do."

"If this leads to a surge in Arthurian converts, I will be mightily vexed with you," Drakeforth said.

We went home and painted the desk's roll top with fresh patchouli oil. Then Drakeforth went to work, pressing his fingers against the panels and slats, massaging the hidden tones. Slowly the entire recording came wafting out on the smell of the herbal vapours. When it was completely released the conversation from over one hundred years earlier went like this:

The Original Huddy Godden: This is remarkable! Who else knows about this?!

Vole's great-great-uncle, Wardrock Drakeforth: *Only the three of us.*

My great-grandfather, Spaniel Pudding: I fear our veil of secrecy will not last long, gentlemen.

Godden: It must. The profit we could make from our discovery!

Pudding: While I agree that we must capitalise on this phenomenon, it should be considered a gift to all mankind.

Godden: It was a wise man who said that three men may keep a secret only when two of them are dead.

Drakeforth: Are you threatening me, Huddy?

Godden: Not at all, Wardrock.

Pudding: Gentlemen. Please...there is glory enough for all in our discovery. We shall publish jointly and share the accolades equally.

Godden: What if we dared to keep this to ourselves? Empathic energy is a living force. We'll need a steady supply of it and we can't just suck it out of people and use it to meet the energy demands of the modern world!

Drakeforth: Indeed we can and so we shall. We take the living essence of our fellow man and imbue it with immortality. We are transferring a degree of their very sentience!

Pudding: It sounds rather ghoulish when you put it like that, Ward.

Godden: No one can ever know of this. Their outrage if they discovered the full potential of double-e flux on the inanimate would get us lynched.

Drakeforth: Spaniel's work has shown we need very little. Just the tiniest amount extracted from a few volunteers. It's enough to imbue anything with greater function.

Godden: Gentlemen, are you familiar with the beliefs of the Arthurians?

Drakeforth: Of course, a collection of gibbering gallbladders intent on wishing themselves into some higher plane of existence.

Pudding: We can extract it from ourselves only. To inflict this process on anyone else would reveal too much.

Godden: Arthurians believe in the ascendance of man into pure energy. I'm sure they could be convinced that we have discovered the path to their nirvana. We get all the double-e flux we require, they get to become one with the universe.

Pudding: You are talking about murder, Godden.

Godden: It's not murder if they volunteer. The real question is, what do we tell the rest of them?

Drakeforth: Them? The great unwashed mob? Tell them it's generated by natural radiation and human emotions.

Godden: Positive human emotions. Our experiments have already shown the risks if we have people acting negatively around empathy-sensitive machinery.

Pudding: We three must swear to never reveal the truth of

where empathic energy comes from. This secret we take it to our graves.

Drakeforth: Long may they stand empty.

The voices faded to silence. We stood together in muteness for a long minute.

"Your great-grandfather, Spaniel Pudding, wanted that conversation to be recorded," Drakeforth said eventually.

"He…" I cleared my throat, "He did seem to have concerns about the plan."

Drakeforth glowered. "And yet he went along with it and turned the world on its head. One hundred years ago? The first buildings powered with empathic energy? The Python building?"

I nodded, "And the cine-plex over in Tytal. A Godden Model Six empathy engine. The empathic energy and sentience of our ancestors has been running those two buildings for nearly a century."

"No wonder they're tired," Drakeforth said.

"If the recorded conversation is true, then the revelation of sentience in empathic engines could have serious consequences," I said.

"The desk and our discoveries about Arthurianism," Drakeforth said and sighed. "That full sentience is only in the oldest engines. Modern technology is so miniaturised you'd barely get a flicker of an actual person out of anything. Besides, all that energy getting churned up together, there's no way you could discern an individual's distinct empathic field."

I stared at the desk, "So no one would care. The worst thing that would happen is that they would replace the empathic resonators in the Python building and put in some new multi-port system to replace great-granddad." Mum and dad were gone. Ascott was alive, but far away, and the thought of losing any aspect of a long-lost relative concerned me.

"Well, it's not like there is anything we can do about it." Drakeforth gestured defeat.

"You're right. We should just forget it. Look, I have to go to work. I've got to explain my absence for the last few days and frankly that's going to take some time."

"Sure, I'll catch up with you later?"

I smiled at Drakeforth, "Yes. I would like that very much." I resisted the silly impulse to kiss him goodbye at the door.

EPILOGUE

I'm leaving this manuscript in the living oak desk, along with great-granddad Pudding's letter. I rang Drakeforth and told him that I was going to an Arthurianist spiritual retreat, and I would like to see him when I returned next week. He accused me of blind bigotry against rational thought and swore that if I returned a blathering convert to such religious quackery he would see me publicly flogged.

I've put a front door key in the post to him, along with a request that he forgive the desk and look after it for me.

The new empathic engine is to be installed at the Python building tomorrow. My body will die tonight, and my complete sentience will be transferred intact into the new machine. They say it will be like going to sleep, and awakening to a thousand new senses beyond description.